REALLY-TRULY Stories

Book 4

By Gwendolen Lampshire Hayden

Illustrated by Vernon Nye

TEACH Services, Inc.
PUBLISHING
www.TEACHServices.com • (800) 367-1844

This book was written to provide truthful information in regard to the subject matter covered. The author assumes full responsibility for the accuracy of all facts and quotations as cited in this book. The opinions expressed in this book are the author's personal views and interpretation of the Bible, Spirit of Prophecy, and/or contemporary authors and do not necessarily reflect those of TEACH Services, Inc.

This book is sold with the understanding that the publisher is not engaged in giving spiritual, legal, medical, or other professional advice. If authoritative advice is needed, the reader should seek the counsel of a competent professional.

Copyright © 2013 TEACH Services, Inc.
ISBN-13: 978-1-4796-0108-0 (Paperback)
ISBN-13: 978-1-4796-0109-7 (ePub)
ISBN-13: 978-1-4796-0110-3 (Kindle/Mobi)

Library of Congress Control Number: 2012955985

Published by

TEACH Services, Inc.
PUBLISHING
www.TEACHServices.com • (800) 367-1844

Table of Contents

Part I
Skip: A Pioneer Boy

Part II
Other Stories

Dedication

This book is appreciatively dedicated to Schuyler (Skip) McClintock Whiting and his sister, Ella Whiting Luckey, whose parents were eastern Oregon pioneers; and to my mother, Grace Brown Lampshire; my aunt, Jessie Linton Moullen; and my uncle, Elbert K. Brown, whose parents were western Oregon pioneers.

> *"Over plains against the sky—*
> *The cloudless, relentless, low-hung sky,*
> *I see them winding wearily by*
> *Bearing a precious human load,*
> *Leaving a cross by the side of a road."*

> *"On down the road I watch them go*
> *Through dust choked clouds that blind and blow;*
> *With the glare of the sun in tired eyes,*
> *But glare of the dream that always lies*
> *Away to the West in sun, filled skies."*

> *—From "The Sunset Trail,"*
> *by permission of Lucia Wilkins Moore.*

Part One

Skip: A Pioneer Boy

Skip Thought It Was Lots of Fun to be a Pioneer

Chapter 1
Prairies and Patches

SKIP STIRRED restlessly, opened his eyes, and sleepily pulled himself into a sitting position on his straw-tick mattress at the end of the big, white-topped wagon. For a moment he sat motionless as his brown eyes blinked at the sprawling forms of his older sister, Lizzie, and two younger brothers, Frank and baby George. He swayed back and forth with the movement of the six horses that plodded heavily along in the chill early-morning air. To the very marrow of his travel-weary bones he felt the tiresome, clumsy rocking of the heavy prairie schooner.

With a lithe, catlike motion he suddenly flung aside his warm patchwork quilt and turned to the wagon's tailboard. His round, inquisitive eyes stared out across the vast, trackless sea of sugar grass, rye grass, and tule, whose ten-foot-tall stems stretched up as far as the high wagon seat where sat pa and ma. At a hoarse, whispered sound beside him he turned quickly to look straight into his sister's brown face.

"Skip, did we eat breakfast? Or have we been riding all night?" she asked in a low voice, fearful of wakening the fretful baby. "I seem to have lost all

9

reckoning of time, traveling the way we are. It just seems months and months since we left Nevada City." She snuggled down under her covers, shivering in the cold air.

"No, we haven't eaten breakfast yet. I 'spect pa and ma started extra early today. They prob'ly decided to let us sleep, planning to stop later on to build a fire and cook breakfast. You know how anxious pa is to get to Rocky Point tonight. He said yesterday that if he had to put one more patch on this wagon or spend one more day on this prairie, he believed the whole outfit'd fall to pieces. It's been a mighty hard trip."

"It sure enough has," soberly agreed Lizzie. "And I hate it, too, every bit of it! I'm not like you, Skip. You think it's fun to be a pioneer and go away off in the wilds somewhere to live. But I downright miss Nevada City and all the houses and all my friends. I wish I were back there right now."

"Well, I don't," stoutly asserted Skip. "I think this is lots more fun. Listen! The folks are talking. Maybe we'll find out when we're going to stop."

"I declare," boomed pa's deep voice, "I never saw such fertile land." The children saw him reach out from the high seat to pull off a bluejoint grass stem waving far above the wagon bed. "No, sir, Ione, I never saw such good land. Why, the soil's been rich like this all the way from the shores of Harney and Malheur lakes. And in all our five hundred miles over the old Emigrant Road I've never seen a sight to equal this one. Thousands of ducks, geese, and birds swarming on those great lakes; countless deer, elk, brown and black bear roaming through

10

this tall sea of prairie grass; and soil that'll grow anything a man'll plant in the ground. Looks as though we'd come to the right place, sure enough."

"Yes, Tom," ma nodded, "I believe the McLeods were right. I'm glad now that they kept writing to Nevada City all this past year, telling us about Rocky Point and urging us to join them. I'll be happy to get there, though. We've been traveling a long time, and I've seen enough strange country to last me the rest of my life."

"Well, I reckon you won't see much more, Ione," pa answered cheerily. "I've a feeling that we're almost at the end of our journey, and that here we'll spend the rest of our natural days. Couldn't find a better spot nowhere."

"Aren't we almost there, Pa?" questioned Skip, raising his shrill voice to make himself heard. As he stared toward the northeast his eyes sparkled, and he suddenly gasped in excitement.

"Oh, look! Look! I see it! I see Rocky Point!" he called.

"Where?" cried Lizzie, scrambling hastily out of bed, forgetful of the sleeping children, who now roused and whimpered fretfully.

"See? 'Way over there," Skip answered. "Look close about that-a-way."

Pa pulled the horses to a stop while they all stared breathlessly in the direction of Skip's pointing finger. Skip was right.

It *was* Rocky Point! Far, far away the little hill breasted the tall, waving sea of green grass as gallantly as ever a small, sturdy ship daringly breasted the green ocean waves.

11

"You're right, boy. You're right!" exclaimed pa. He clambered quickly down the great wagon wheel and then turned to hold up his arms for ma. Lizzie expertly gathered up the squalling George and handed him down to ma.

"Everybody dressed and out of the wagon," pa said firmly. "We'll stop right now and build a fire for breakfast. Everybody's hungry, and this is as good a place to make camp as any. Better cook up some extra victuals so's we can have something ready to eat on the way. Reckon this'll be the last meal stop until we get to McLeods'. Lizzie, you help your ma while Skip and I tend to the horses."

How good the fire felt, and how good the hot, frying-pan bread, boiled potatoes, and codfish tasted! The children ate ravenously, stuffing themselves until ma vowed that they could not hold another bite. Then Skip and Frank ran back and forth, round and round the wagon, glad of a chance to stretch their cramped legs. Lizzie, secretly wishing that she, too, could spend the time playing, pretended to sniff scornfully at their puppy-like romping. She set her red lips in a prim line as she busily helped ma wash and put away the breakfast dishes and pack the remainder of the food in the big, iron-bound grub box.

"It's your turn," yelled Skip, as he charged out from the thick rye grass. "Hurry up, Frankie. Now see if you can hide so's I can't find you. Quick, now, if you want to play. Pa'll soon be ready to start. Here. I'll close my eyes until you call 'Ready.'"

He turned, hid his face on his raised arm, and waited until he heard his small brother's voice,

12

faint and far away.

"Re—a—dy. I'm all re—a—dy."

"Don't go far from camp, children," cautioned pa. "Better stay around pretty close. You must remember that this is a wild, unsettled country. We're likely to run onto any kind of critter, and some of them can be mighty unfriendly."

"All right, Pa," Skip answered on the run, only half listening to his father's advice. "Come on, Liz, help me find Frank," begged Skip. He dashed off in the direction whence his brother's little voice had called. "We'll have to hurry. Pa's going to harness the horses pretty soon."

"Here we come," chanted Skip and Lizzie. "Here we come, on the run." Feeling like mighty hunters in a dense green jungle, they scurried here and there through the tall grasses that waved high above their heads. On and on, round and round in circles they ran, shouting and panting for breath. But no small voice answered them.

At last they stopped and looked at each other with round, frightened eyes. It had been some time since they had heard pa's or ma's voices. Far back in the distance ma had called their full names, and they knew that ma never used their full names unless she was frightened or angry, or unless she was politely introducing them to a stranger.

"Ione! Ione Elizabeth Schuyler! Schuyler McClintock. Frank! Frank Talbot. Where are you? Where are you?"

Pa's voice too had sounded weak and far away. "Lizzie. Skip. Frankie. Where are you? Answer me. Where are you?" His big booming voice had been muffled. They could not tell from which direction it had come.

Although their hearts thumped painfully and they breathed in deep gasps, they again began to run—on and on and on into the nowhere of the tall green grasses—until they were forced to halt. Their ears ached to hear a familiar voice, but only the vast silence answered them. With sinking hearts Skip and Lizzie realized that they were lost. Little Frank was lost, too, somewhere in this waving forest of sugar grass, rye grass, and tule. They were lost on the vast, level, unknown prairie.

Lizzie caught tight hold of Skip's grimy hands. She held her head high and tried to speak bravely, but Skip saw telltale tears in her eyes and heard her voice quaver. "What shall we do, Skip? I don't know which way to go. Do you?"

"No, Liz, I really don't," Skip answered stoutly, though with a sinking heart. "But one thing sure we'll have to depend on ourselves, just like pa said. We'll have to act like real pioneers now and try to figure how to get out of here. We've got to figure out something, because pa said when he hobbled the horses that he wouldn't be able to see their backs if they got loose out here, so we know he can't see us either.

"I reckon we'd better wait right here. If we move we may just wander farther away from camp. I do wish I'd listened to pa. And I-I wish we'd brought Shep with us. He'd have known the way back, all right."

Lizzie's tear-filled eyes brightened hopefully. "Skip! Let's scream as loud as we can. Maybe

Shep'll be close enough to hear us even if pa and ma can't. If he is, he'll come running. Then we'll be all right."

Quickly the two children faced in opposite directions, screaming loudly. Again and again they stretched their mouths wide and shouted until their tired voices were hoarse and their throats sore. And at last, just as they turned despairingly toward each other, they heard a series of shrill barks that rapidly grew louder and louder.

"Good old Shep," they cried. "Good old dog. Come here, Shep. Come on, good old dog." They jumped up and down, looking anxiously this way and that through the tangled grasses.

Closer and closer came the barking Shep until at last he burst through the prairie wilderness and leaped joyfully upon them. It was just at that happy moment that they heard a scream of pure terror.

"It's Frank!" gasped Lizzie. "Listen." Again they heard the little boy's pitiful wail.

"He's over there," Skip said, his tanned cheeks paling. "Here, Shep. Go to him. Go to Frankie."

"Oh, what do you s'pose is wrong?" Lizzie sobbed jerkily as they ran pell-mell after Shep, heedless of the sharp grasses that slashed painfully across their faces and hands.

At last they burst breathlessly into a tiny, half-open spot. They were just in time to find Frank sobbing in terror while Shep leaped after an ugly, slinking gray beast. They stood horrified as the strange, snarling creature stopped for an instant and turned its blazing yellow eyes toward them. Then it melted away into the grass until only the vaguest outline could be seen, driven from the small clearing by the ferocious growls of the stiff-legged Shep.

"Liz, Liz, I'm s-s-scared!" wailed little Frank through chattering teeth. He stumbled toward them, his face white and tear stained. Lizzie met him halfway and clutched him tightly in her arms. "I'm afraid, Liz. I want ma," he sobbed, flinging his little arms around her neck.

"Sh-h-h. Shh, Frankie. We're all right now," she soothed, at the same time casting a terrified glance toward the place where the big wild animal had so recently stood snarling at them.

And then all of a sudden everything was all right. "Lizzie. Skip. Frank. I'm coming. Pa's coming." First the children heard the sweet sound of pa's strong voice.

Then there was a sound like thunder as pa's muzzle-loading rifle boomed over their heads. And

An Ugly Gray Beast Melted Away Into the Tall Grass

16

suddenly there wasn't even the faintest outline of that awful beast across the clearing. Only faithful Shep was left with them in the half-open circle.

"Missed!" exclaimed pa in disgust. "I should have hit that critter dead center. Guess I was too excited."

The children ran toward him, rejoicing in his nearness and his strength. "O pa, what was it?" cried Lizzie, wiping away her tears on her stained calico apron.

Pa smiled down at Lizzie and Skip as he reached out and took the limp Frankie from Lizzie's tired arms.

Pa slowly shook his head. "I don't rightly know," he said. "Could have been a coyote or maybe even a timber wolf. Anyway, it's a mighty good thing I sent Shep after you when I did, for that varmint looked like a mean customer to me. But all's well that ends well, and you're all safe and sound, with nothing worse than a few scratches and a bad scare. When I heard all the commotion I was mighty afeard that I might have to put some patches on you children, same as I've been doing to make the wagon hold together. And I've about run out of patches."

His kind eyes twinkled happily down at them. Skip and Lizzie began to lose the tight ache in their throats, and little Frank gave a tired sigh and leaned his head against pa's shoulder. It didn't seem half so far going back to the camp as it had seemed running away from it. And it was good to have ma hurry to greet them and give each of them a thankful kiss.

They were all very quiet as they settled down in their accustomed places in the big wagon to resume the last part of their journey. Baby George was already asleep. Soon Lizzie and Frank closed their eyes. And after a while Skip's head began to nod. Over and over in his ears rang the singsong refrain of the many places that they had seen along the way—Nevada City, California, Oregon, Warner Lake, Mule Springs, Buzzard Canyon, Double OO, Weaver Springs, Venator Ranch, Old Emigrant Trail, Harney Lake, Malheur Lake. He wondered when they would reach Rocky Point. Again in his thoughts the names began to go round and round: Nevada City, California, Oregon—

"Welcome! Welcome to Rocky Point," two cheery voices sang out. Skip's head straightened with a painful jerk. He stared dazedly before he realized the truth. At last their big wagon had rolled to a stop in front of the lone house. Their long journey had ended. At last they had arrived safely at Rocky Point!

"Why, Skip, how you've grown! And you, too, Lizzie, and Frank. Here's the new baby too. Bless his heart." Mrs. McLeod reached hungry arms for little George and cradled him close against her.

"But come now, good friends. It's almost dark. No more talking until you've had a chance to wash and eat supper. I know how tired of camp cooking you must be, for I made that same trip last year. Come right this way. I've got lots of hot water on the stove. You children can clean up out at the wash bench while your pa tends to his horses. Then by the time he comes in I'll have the supper dished up and steaming on the table."

All of them ate a great deal of the delicious home-cooked food, but Skip ate until he thought he would burst. The quantities of boiled beef and potatoes, corn bread and wild currant jelly, and dried-peach pie vanished like snowflakes on a red-hot griddle. Everything tasted good to the hungry, weary travelers.

At last Skip's head dropped lower and lower. His black hair fell forward into his almost empty plate and his freckled nose pressed against the last bite of dried-peach pie. He could not remember ma removing his outer garments or pa carrying him out to the bed in the wagon. But he smiled happily in his sleep as, in a half-dream, he heard pa's deep voice speak gently:

"Sleep well, my brave boy. Sleep well. Tomorrow we begin our new home in this great valley. Sweet dreams, Skip, our boy pioneer."

"Well, Folks," Said Pa Happily, "We're Safe at Home in Our Rocky Point Dugout!"

Chapter 2
Dugout Days

COME, COME, children. It's time to get up. I've let you sleep much later than usual this morning. It's past six o'clock and breakfast's almost ready. Ma's already fed the baby. Hurry now, so you won't keep Mrs. McLeod waiting. There's work a-plenty for each of us today." Pa's deep voice boomed through the flap over the wagon's tailboard.

Skip stretched and blinked his sleepy eyes. Then he reluctantly threw back the warm wool covers, reached for his cold-stiffened outer garments, and shiveringly dragged them on over the long red flannel underwear in which he had slept.

"Br-r-r! It's cold," he mumbled through chattering teeth to Lizzie, humped like a cross legged Indian squaw beneath her miniature bedding-tent. "It isn't winter yet, but it sure feels mighty like it's just around the corner."

"Well, after all, this is October, and pa says that this valley's altitude is almost five thousand feet," Lizzie said in a chill little voice. Skip saw that her breath rose like steam from beneath her covers. "That's why pa's got to hurry and get our dugout ready before the ground's frozen hard or covered with snow. He's in a hurry to get us into our winter quarters so's he can make that long trip to Canyon City to get our supplies."

"Why does pa have to go so far away to buy food, Lizzie?" questioned little Frank, as he pulled on the tiny cowboy boots made exactly like Skip's. "Why couldn't pa bring all our food with us in the wagon from Nevada City?"

"Why, because we were all riding in the wagon, Frankie boy, and there wasn't an inch of extra space left over. And now that we're here we're miles and miles from any town. There aren't any stores nearer than Canyon City, and Mr. McLeod says that's seventy-five miles. So pa'll have to go there and bring back supplies enough to last us until next spring. The McLeods are the only folks living here on Rocky Point, and they don't have enough to share with this big family."

"Children!" Ma's voice called cheerily through the early morning darkness from the hastily opened kitchen door of the McLeods' frame house.

"Come on," urged Skip. "I'm starved." With one accord they tumbled out and hurried to the house, where they hastily washed and then sat down to a hot breakfast of sourdough biscuits, codfish boiled with potatoes, fried steak, and gravy.

Then while ma helped Mrs. McLeod with the dishes and housework, and Lizzie took care of the cross baby and little Frank, Mr. McLeod, pa, and Skip put on their heavy wraps and went out into the crisp morning air. Mr. McLeod led the way around the brow of the low hill. "I've been doin' some lookin' beforehand, and it 'pears to me that the most likely spot for your place is 'bout here," he said as he stopped at the crest of the hill and pointed to a trail that led down the gentle slope. "Just about down there aways is a good spot for diggin'. There's solid rock beneath and yet it's high enough to be out of danger in case of flood water come spring thaw and breakup. It ain't far for carryin' drinkin' water either, and, all in all, it's the likeliest spot I've found hereabouts."

"I think you're dead right, Frank," agreed Tom Whiting, nodding his head. "You've done well to choose such a convenient place. Now the thing to do is to get right to work. We'll go get our pick-ax and shovels, and make that dirt fairly fly. Next summer I'll go upriver and cut some of those fine pine logs you told me about. I'll float 'em down the Silvies River, and build a log cabin somewhere near here. But right now, with old man Winter breathin' down our necks, we'll make out with this dugout cut back into the hillside. I'll guarantee we'll be as snug as any bear in his den."

Busy days followed. All during the daylight hours the two men, Skip, and sometimes Lizzie worked hard in the pale wintry sunlight. The first snowflakes had whirled down and whitened the frozen ground before pa and Mr. McLeod leaned wearily on their dirt-encrusted shovels and looked about with tired smiles of satisfaction. But Skip and Lizzie jumped excitedly into the air and whooped wild whoops of glee. At their loud shouts ma and Mrs. McLeod hurried out of the warm kitchen into the frosty air, hugging their coats and shawls close about them.

"Well, Ione," said pa. "Here's your new house, all ready to move into. How do you like it?"

Anxiously the children and pa watched ma as she looked carefully at the dugout top, securely covered with lumber scraps and straw. They followed closely as she stepped inside the large cave and inspected the rock-lined sidewalls, the hard-packed dirt floor, the rough table and cupboards, and the snug bunks waiting for their straw mattresses and woolen quilts. They watched eagerly as she eyed the newly polished, cast-iron, four-lidded cookstove sitting chummily beside the small, new, rock fireplace. Skip and Lizzie let out long, relieved breaths as she smiled at all of them and spoke briskly.

"I declare, Tom, I believe it's going to be real cozy in spite of the fact that there are no windows and only one door. You've all worked hard and have done well. The next thing to do is to put my braided rugs down on the floor. They'll help keep our feet warm. Then we'll make up the beds. After that we'll bring in our dishes and food supplies, and hang our clothes on the wall pegs. It looks as though tonight we'll really be at home in Rocky Point."

"Just in time, too," remarked Mr. McLeod. "A regular storm's goin' to blow up before tomorrow, or I'll miss my guess." He stepped to the dugout doorway and squinted at the leaden sky. "Yep, she's a-goin' to storm, sure enough. We timed it just right, Tom. Looks like an early winter's settin' in."

"Well, all I can say is that I hope it doesn't start too early," pa announced, with a worried frown creasing his tanned forehead. "I've still got that long trip to Canyon City after supplies. We've got to have those things—there's no two ways about it!"

"Oh, you'll make it safe enough," Mr. McLeod answered. "I wish I could have hauled enough for all of us when I went across the mountains last month, but that Blue Mountain grade's too steep for a double load. However, just give this first storm a few days to blow itself out, and then when it freezes good and solid you'll be all right. Only thing, though, you'd better watch your horses pretty close from now on. As soon as the snows drift deep the timber wolves'll get starved out up in the hills. Then they're apt to come down real close."

Wolves! Skip and Lizzie looked at each other with wide-open eyes as shivers of fright ran up and down their chilly backs.

"Did-did you ever see a wolf here—right here at Rocky Point, Mr. McLeod?" questioned Skip, scarcely daring to breathe as he waited for an answer.

"That's right, boy. I shore did. Killed two big timber wolves last winter—in fact, not far from where you're standin' right now."

Skip and Lizzie moved hastily and glanced over their shoulders, half expecting to see two big, gray, furry figures slinking close behind them, with eyes gleaming red, tongues lolling hungrily between sharp, white teeth.

"You needn't be afeard, though," Mr. McLeod chuckled. "Them two wolves won't ever bother anyone again. And the rest of 'em that are runnin' around in the timber won't come near anyone in the daytime unless they're powerful hungry. But by that time they'll be down so close to us that you'll hear 'em a-howlin' at night and have plenty of warnin' that they're near. We'll get out my steel wolf traps soon. Then we'll be ready if the varmints pay us a visit."

The afternoon hours winged by as the two families plodded back and forth, carrying supplies from the big white-topped wagon into the hillside dugout. Lizzie helped ma spread the cold muslin sheets over the plumped-up straw mattresses and tuck in the warm wool quilts securely at the bunk edges.

"Next fall we'll have some real mattresses," ma said. "Mrs. McLeod has two of the best wool mattresses I've ever seen, and she's told me where I can get some."

"But wouldn't they be awfully expensive?" queried practical Lizzie. "And where can you buy wool mattresses in this country, with no store closer than seventy-five miles?"

"Just you wait and see, my girl. But have them we will, and there'll be none finer anywhere." Ma smiled mysteriously as she smoothed down the last patchwork coverlet and turned to finish hanging up the clothing. She spread a braided rug over the big clothing chest and stepped back to view her work.

"There!" ma said in a satisfied tone. "If anyone'd told me when I was a girl back in Ohio that I'd come around the Horn, meet your pa in California, and come to Oregon to live in a dugout—I'd have said he was out of his mind. But here we are! And snug and warm and settled for the winter. We've much to be thankful for."

The two of them hurried to the McLeod house to find the rest of the family all ready for the tasty early supper that Mrs. McLeod had prepared for the weary workers. And then, with their cheery, heartfelt thanks ringing in the frosty air the Whiting family hurried to their dugout home. Quickly the two tired younger children were tucked into bed, after saying their prayers, and fell asleep almost as soon as their weary little heads touched the soft down pillows. Pa hurried outside for just one more armload of wood and for a last look at his horses, huddled close together in the crude shelter near by.

Ma put her arms around Skip and Lizzie, and drew them close. For a rare, still moment they stood motionless, looking about them in the purpling dusk. In the dugout home all was nearness and order—all was quietness except for the occasional snap of a red spark from the stove's front eyelets or the sharper crackle of the gnarled mahogany logs that burned brightly in the fireplace.

Skip glanced contentedly around, feeling the safeness and tenderness of ma's embrace. Close beside him the homemade chairs sat around the rough table, with its neat red-and-white checked tablecloth and its round-bellied coal-oil lamp. Ma's hit-and-miss rugs gleamed brightly in the slanting firelight that danced across the floor and flickered rosily on ma and pa's battered rockers and grandma's old spinning wheel in the far corner.

They heard the sharp sound of rapid footsteps on the hard-frozen earth as pa walked quickly along the path and flung open the stout door. He hurried inside with one last load of long-burning mahogany wood, and deftly dropped it on top of the neatly stacked woodpile before he turned to fasten the door. Before it slammed shut they caught one final glimpse of the vast, silent valley lying mutely beneath the millions of glittering stars that gleamed coldly in the night sky arching far, far overhead.

"Well, folks, we're home," said pa happily. "We're safe at home in our Rocky Point dugout and snug as snug can be. Just in time, too, for winter's almost here." A long, mournful howl floated eerily across the distant snowy miles of grass and sagebrush, mahogany and pine. Shep's shaggy head lifted from his outstretched paws and a low answering growl rumbled in his throat.

"A timber wolf!" Skip and Lizzie spoke at once. Lizzie clutched pa's iron-muscled arm, but Skip stood alone and stiffly erect. Pa looked quickly at ma's whitening face as he nodded his head.

"It *is* a wolf, for certain, but he's a long, long ways from Rocky Point. Nothing's going to harm us here, folks. You've done your work well, and now we're secure and safe from all harm outside."

Skip felt a shiver of delightful anticipation that mingled and blended with his prickling scalp. Here they were, all of them, living in a real hillside home and listening to real winter wolves baying at the cold, pale moon.

Again he glanced happily about. On the shelf the old pendulum clock ticked on and on, ticking out the old, ticking in the new. Skip knew deep in his heart that many exciting dugout days lay ahead.

Chapter 3
Winter and Wolves

SKIP STOPPED abruptly just outside the dugout's partially opened door. Through its inchwide crack he stared as he saw his mother place her work roughened hand on pa's coat sleeve and heard her pleading voice as she looked up into his bearded face.

"I know we'll get along all right, Tom. McLeods are real close by to help if anything goes wrong and, of course, Lizzie'll be here with me. It's you I'm worried about. I just can't bear the thought of you making that long trip all alone. I'd feel much better knowing that Skip was with you. He's only a boy, to be sure, but he's brave and reliable. If anything *should* happen he could ride for help."

Ma's soft voice quavered as she finished speaking, and pa's cheery tones sounded extra loud by contrast as he quickly answered. "Why, Ione, to think you'd worry about me. Nothing's happened to *me* yet, and I believe that any man who's weathered the ups and downs of the '49 gold rush and got out with a whole skin's not apt to have any serious trouble on a trip over the Blue Mountains.

"To tell the truth, I'd thought some of taking the boy along so he could see that part of the country.

But I'd about decided he'd better stay here with you while I'm away. I'll see, though."

Skip's heart thumped loudly as he moved back a few steps. He waited several minutes before he puckered up his lips and began to whistle loudly to announce his approach as he again neared the door. He hadn't meant to eavesdrop, but now that he had accidentally overheard ma's wish for tomorrow he couldn't help being glad. All during the week-long preparations for pa's trip he had been secretly wishing and longing that he, too, could go, but he had not dared ask. He had been sure that ma would need him here at Rocky Point. But now his cheeks flushed red and his eyes blazed with excitement as he realized that he might be a passenger in the big wagon when it set forth in the blackness of early dawn.

All during supper he hugged the precious secret hope close to him while he waited impatiently for pa to speak. But it was not until ma had put away the supper dishes, Lizzie had emptied the dishwater outside, and all the family had gathered around the cheery warmth of the fireplace that pa actually spoke to him about the journey.

"Well, son, it looks as though I'm due to have a partner on my Canyon City trip if your ma has her way. She thinks I'd better take you with me—sort of for protection, I reckon. Guess she thinks that if I got clawed by a bear or fell and broke a leg, you could ride one of the horses back here for help. How about it? It'll be a long, cold trip. Do you want to go along?"

As pa's merry eyes twinkled first at ma and then at him, Skip felt his throat choke up with a sudden rush of joy that left him speechless. All he could do was to nod his head and blink the sudden moisture from his eyes. "Just think! I'm going with pa. Do you s'pose we'll see any wild animals on the way—bears or catamounts or timber wolves?" he whispered to Lizzie, sleepily curled in the adjoining bunk.

"I don't know. I'd say that you're apt to see most anything in this wilderness. But right now you'd better settle down to get some rest. Morning'll come pretty sudden."

"Oh, I'm too excited to settle down," he retorted, turning restlessly from left to right and from right to left. "I know I won't sleep a wink all night."

However, it seemed that only the next moment pa was shaking his shoulder and saying, "Get up, son. Get up. It's three o'clock, and time for breakfast. We've got a long day ahead of us."

Skip staggered drowsily to his feet and hurriedly dressed in his warmest clothing. He watched as ma quietly moved back and forth between the cookstove and the table, heaping their plates with golden brown sour dough biscuits and gravy. They spoke in low voices, careful not to awaken Lizzie, Frank, and George.

"Eat all you can," warned ma. "It'll be some time before you sit down to a table again." She worked even while she talked, packing more and more food into the big grub box on one corner of the table and checking and rechecking the shopping list before she handed it to pa. "How long do you think you'll be gone, Tom?"

"Can't rightly say, Ione. It shouldn't be too long, though, according to what McLeod tells me about

31

the trip. Of course, he made it earlier in the year, when the ground was clear. Being it's November now, we may strike some deep snow on up the canyons. If we do, that'll slow us up considerable."

"Well, do be careful," ma admonished. "You've got your wagon full of grain and hay for the horses and food and bedding for yourselves, so you should be all right. Oh, here's one last thing. I almost forgot about it." Ma knelt quickly to open the oven door with her apron-protected hand.

"I'll get them, Ma," Skip said hurriedly. He grabbed a towel, took out the two well-heated rocks, and carefully folded them in two small rugs.

"Mm-mm. They'll feel mighty good at our feet. Thanks, Ma," he said gratefully, giving her a quick, boyish kiss before he picked up the foot warmers and carried them out to the waiting wagon.

"Indeed they will, son, for I see that the weather's turning clear and colder. Now be sure that your pa remembers to heat them up each night in the overnight campfire. I've always said that a body can stand almost anything in freezing weather as long as he's got a place to warm his feet and hands. You've got warmth for your feet. Now here's warmth for your hands."

Ma reached far back into the oven and pulled out four hot baked potatoes. Smiling, she dropped two of them into Skip's coat pockets and two of them into pa's coat pockets. Then she kissed pa and Skip, and, throwing a woolly shawl over her head and shoulders, stood in the lamp-lighted doorway to wave good-by. As the big wagon moved creakingly away in the darkness, Skip kept turning to look back until ma's figure grew smaller and smaller and at last vanished from sight.

"Do you really think we'll have any trouble, pa?" questioned Skip anxiously as the horses plodded on and on over the ice-crusted snow. "Ma seemed real worried about our trip. I don't see why, though. Surely no wild animals would attack us, and there aren't any Indians around here now since the Paiutes went away to Pyramid Lake."

"Well, I'm not anticipatin' any trouble, son," answered pa in his slow, deep voice. "I aim to be careful, though, so's we don't have any bad mishaps. When a man's as far from civilization as we are it pays him to be extra cautious, for he's got only himself to depend on, just like the pioneers who came West over twenty years ago. That's what was worryin' your ma.

"In a way we're pioneers, too—comin' up to this new, unsettled land where there's no doctor closer than seventy-five miles and only a handful of settlers scattered over thousands and thousands of acres of unclaimed land. This is a right big valley for only fifteen people to fill. So far we're just pinpoints on the surface, but the day'll come when other folks'll hear about this land. Then we'll have more neighbors and a town right on Rocky Point and a school for all you youngsters. We can be good neighbors to these new folks as they come, and help them get settled, just as the McLeods helped us.

"Yes, sir, I aim to be right careful all the way over and back," pa repeated firmly as his gloved hand brushed the frozen moisture from his beard.

"Your ma's dependin' on the Lord to help us, and I reckon He will; but I've always believed the Lord helps them as helps themselves, and I aim to live up to my part of the partnership."

Skip never forgot that bitterly cold, snowy journey in the early winter of 1874, as they climbed up, up into the timbered slopes of the Blue Mountains. When they reached Soda Springs, a distance of fifty miles from Rocky Point, the temperature had dropped to 60 degrees below. Deep snow forced them to stop and build a bobsled upon which to place the wagon bed, leaving the wheels for their return journey.

Each night they built a blazing campfire, both for warmth and for protection. As soon as they made camp Skip dragged in ample wood supplies to feed the greedy flames through the night. He always remembered to heat the rocks that ma had given them. With the comforting warmth of this bed warmer Skip snuggled under his blankets and quilts in the big wagon. As he listened shiveringly to the eerie, laughing barks of the moon-mad prairie coyotes and the full-throated baying of the wolf pack as it closed in upon its luckless winter kill, he was thankful that strong, dependable pa slept close by his side.

After many weary days of travel they reached the tiny settlement of Canyon City, nestled deep between tall mountains at the entrance to John Day Valley. It was here that they could purchase the necessary supplies brought in by pack train over the difficult two-hundred-mile trail from The Dalles, Oregon. Prices were high, for many of the

Skip Would Never Forget That Bitterly Cold, Snowy Journey as They
Climbed Up, Up, Into the Timbered Slopes of the Blue Mountains

articles were carried in on the bent backs of hardy miners.

Skip stared in fascination at the motley groups passing along the one main street of the gold-mining center: red-shirted miners, black-coated "gentlemen of fortune," pigtailed Chinamen, smooth-faced fortune-hunting boys with six-shooters strapped about their waists. While Skip listened open-mouthed to the many intermingled conversations in the big general store, pa brought out ma's neatly written list. They loaded their wagon with the many items so necessary for the long winter months: John Day apples, fifty-pound sacks of flour, Golden Sea light-brown sugar, salt, matches in five-gallon cans, green coffee beans that would later be parched in the oven and ground fine in ma's coffee mill, potatoes, dried onions, dried codfish, a fifty-pound sack of dried apples for ma's good sauce and pies. Pa checked and rechecked each item to see that nothing was omitted: Lindsey-woolsey for winter garments, calico dress goods at one dollar a yard for summer dresses, red flannel for winter underwear and sleepers, heavy muslin for summer undergarments, rickrack braid trimming and, especially, coal oil, even though the exorbitant cost was 75 cents for one small tin.

Pa looked up and nodded his head in reply to the storekeeper's question before he moved to the far end of the counter to make additional purchases. When Skip returned from carrying out the last coal oil can he found the friendly storekeeper carefully laying aside yards and yards of pretty white calico with a pattern of dainty blue buds. This he placed with heavy black grosgrain silk dress material of equal yardage. He carefully wrapped them in a large bundle and handed them to pa.

"There you are, Mr. Whiting, and thank you very much. I hope you get home safe and sound, and that you'll he hack again next year after the spring thaw." He leaned across the counter and handed Skip a couple of delicious soda crackers with a generous slab of cheese.

Pa answered pleasantly, Skip thanked the store. keeper, and then they turned to leave the general store with its mingled odors of cheese, pickles, dried fish, boots, leather goods, and kerosene.

"Why did you buy all that material, Pa?" queried Skip. "I looked over ma's list, too, and I didn't see anything about white calico or silk grosgrain."

Pa's eyes fairly danced as he smiled down at Skip. But he only shook his head as he answered, "Son, there's a time for telling what you know, and there's a time for keeping silent. Now you pretend real hard that you've never seen what's in that big bundle and whatever you do, don't mention it to your ma. Just remember that Christmas is comin' next month, and I want to have a little surprise or two tucked away. So mind now and keep quiet."

"Christmas!" exclaimed Skip. "Why, that's right; it'll soon be December." As he climbed into the wagon he wondered what he could get for ma. There wasn't any extra money to spend or a way to earn any now. But in spite of this unsolved problem he could not help wondering curiously what other unseen articles might be tucked away somewhere in their purchases. A delightful little glow of pleasant anticipation warmed him as he thought that just possibly one of those carefully tied packages might be for him. But he pressed his lips tight together and asked no further questions.

They slowly and carefully made the icy return journey. When they reached Soda Springs they removed the sled runners and again put on the big wheels that previously had been left there.

It was late on the afternoon of the fortieth day after their departure when they first saw the little rounded knoll of Rocky Point with a welcoming blue curl of smoke rising straight from the chimney of the McLeod house and a smaller wisp rising from their dugout chimney.

"Yoo-hoo!" yelled Skip as they neared the hill. He stood up by the high wagon seat, cupped his mittened hands around his mouth, and called again and again. "Yoo-hoo, Ma! Here we are. We're home!"

Suddenly the dugout door opened. Out ran Lizzie, hair streaming behind her hood. Frank followed close on her heels, screaming with joy. Then ma appeared quickly in the doorway, holding the shawl-bundled George. Last to hurry toward them were their good friends, the McLeods.

Then for a time all was excitement as they exchanged happy greetings and unloaded many of the supplies. After pa had stabled and cared for the tired horses he hurried into the welcome warmth of the dugout. Everyone exclaimed over the extra treat of the expensive soda crackers and the few cans of peaches, plums, and pears that pa bought for the two families.

"O Tom, you shouldn't have bought them," ma gasped; but Skip saw her gay smile as she looked first at pa, then at the crackers and fruit, and then back at pa.

"Nothing's too good for my family and friends," pa replied, putting his arm around ma's slender waist and holding her close to him. "And it's right good to be home again. All the way over and back I kept thinking about each one of you, and wondering if all was well here at Rocky Point."

"Why, we got along just fine," answered ma in her calm, quiet voice. "After all, no harm could befall us with Lizzie here to help me and with the McLeods right next door."

"I thought maybe you'd be fighting off an Indian attack. Or perhaps the wolves might have come swooping down around the house and plagued you," pa teased lightheartedly, glad clear to the tips of his sturdy boots that they were safe at home.

"Well, now, Tom," drawled Mr. McLeod, "you're dead wrong about the Injuns but not far wrong about the wolves a swoopin' down. I trapped one three nights back. Seems we had some venison hangin' on the porch overnight. The next mornin' we found big tracks around both the house and the dugout, so I decided to put out a trap right then and there. Warned the youngsters to watch out fer it—them steel jaws are mighty powerful and told 'em not to set a foot outside after dark. Looks as though all the game's comin' down into the valley to winter feed, and of course the hungry varmints are comin' right along after 'em, since there's nothin' much left up in the hills for 'em to eat."

Skip saw pa's laughing face sober quickly as he stepped over to the wall and took down the muzzle-loading rifle that he had just brought in from the wagon. He looked the mechanism over closely, even though he knew it to be in perfect working condition, and then rehung it on its wall pegs.

"I aim to be ready if and when they come again," he said grimly. "No wild beast's going to do any harm around here—not if I can help it."

"Do you think any more wolves will come back?" Skip asked breathlessly, a plan flashing instantly into his mind. "Could we set another trap near the dugout? How I'd like to catch one of those big fellows."

"Br-r-r," shivered Lizzie. "You wouldn't want even to get near one if you'd seen the teeth and the claws on the one that was caught."

"He shore was monstrous big," Mr. McLeod affirmed. "But the skin'll make a fine rug for our bedroom floor when it's properly tanned and lined. My wife's wanted a warm rug for quite a spell, so I guess this hungry wolf's goin' to serve one good purpose."

Skip stared at Mr. McLeod with wistful eyes. He felt that his good friend must have read his unspoken wish, for suddenly Mr. McLeod said, "Come along, Skip. Want to come outside with me just a minute? You can give me some help." As soon as they were outside and had shut the door behind them Mr. McLeod continued:

"We'll reset the trap right near your dugout roof. The dead wolf's mate is sure to come here sooner or later and get caught. In that case there'll be another hide to tan—one that you can give to your mother for a Christmas present. How'll that be?"

Skip was so excited that his hands trembled as Mr. McLeod showed him how to arrange the bait and set the jaws of the big steel trap. All evening long, as the family sat in the dugout's cozy warmth, he listened to the faraway wolf howls, hoping desperately that the pack would come nearer and nearer. Even after he went to bed he determined to stay awake to find out. Then he would be sure to hear the spring of the huge trap if the dead wolf's mate came near. But even as he finished the thought he fell sound asleep.

Not once during the night did he stir or waken, not even when his parents roused and talked in low voices concerning the mournful wails of the winter wolves. He did not hear his father get up and hastily dress as the eerie desert symphony's crescendo grew louder and louder; nor did he hear him go outside to calm the frightened, trembling horses.

It was not until he awoke the next morning, pulled on his clothing, and rushed outside that he found that his dearest wish had come true. For there, securely trapped near the bait, lay a huge gray timber wolf, lured to his death by his own greed.

"We got him! We got him! Come quick and see," Skip yelled. In his excitement he jumped up and down. "Come on, Lizzie, look at the wolf. Hurry."

"I'm coming!" shrieked Lizzie, struggling with her high-laced shoes. "I'll be there in just a minute."

Pa hurried up the pathway, smiling a broad smile. "That's right, son; you really caught your wolf, for a fact. And a right fine rug he'll make for your ma's Christmas present too. McLeod told me about your plans, and Mrs. McLeod said she'd fix a good lining for the under part after I got it tanned. Your ma'll be real surprised when she finds out the pelt's for her.

"I heard him in the night, so I came up here with my gun and finished him. I don't like to see any critter suffer needlessly, even if it's an ornery, thievin', murderin' varmint like this timber wolf. Yes sir, son, I think this'll be a mighty fine present for ma. Don't you?"

Skip nodded proudly as he stood beside the dead wolf and looked out across the valley, far across the wide, snowy miles to the distant, snow-capped Blue Mountains. He thought of the long winter journey to get the supplies, of the many good visits that he and pa had had by the nightly campfires, of the interesting sights of Canyon City, of their safe return. His heart swelled with happiness.

"Yes, Pa," he said. He wanted to say something more, but from shyness the words stuck in his throat. He wished that he could tell pa how much he loved this wilderness life with its thrilling adventures and its constant demand for manliness and bravery, kindness and generosity. But as he looked up into pa's kind face he knew that pa understood.

Chapter 4
Christmas at Rocky Point

THE CHILDREN'S eyes flew wide open the very instant that pa rattled the stove lids. Skip and Lizzie did not have to be called that morning. For just a moment they snuggled down under their warm covers as they savored the delicious thought that tonight—this very night—was Christmas Eve.

"My!" exclaimed ma in surprise as they both hurried out of bed and shivered into their clothing. "Are you children getting up now?"

"Oh, yes, Ma, we couldn't sleep another wink if we tried," cried Lizzie. "Just think! Tonight is Christmas Eve. I can hardly wait."

"Wait? Wait for what?" questioned pa. "I don't know of anything special that's going to happen tonight, do you, Ma?" His voice sounded stern and almost cross, but Lizzie and Skip saw his eyes twinkle as he turned toward the fireplace.

"Now, Tom," ma laughed. "Don't tease them. They've set their hearts on their Christmas plans. It carries me back to the time I was a child in Ohio. Those were wonderful days." For just an instant Skip saw the laughter go out of her face and a look of wistful longing take its place. But then the smile came back as she looked at them in her same loving way. Skip felt a wave of happiness sweep warmly over him as he thought how her face would light up when he gave her the wonderful present that was all ready and waiting at McLeods' house.

The old pendulum clock swiftly tick-tocked away the morning hours and the early afternoon hours. But then its hands seemed to lag. Skip looked intently at its cracked face as he put another kettle of snow on the stove's reddened lids. "Look at the time again, Lizzie," he called as he paused outside the dugout door. "I'm going up to McLeods' for a few minutes, and I'll ask them the time. I think our clock's run down."

"The clock's all right. You're the one who's slowing down, Skip," ma laughed. "Hurry along, now, but don't be gone very long. We want to get our baths out of the way so that we can have an early supper tonight. McLeods are coming down here to spend Christmas Eve, you know, and then we'll have Christmas Day dinner with them tomorrow. You and pa'll have to hurry to get the chores out of the way. We want a long evening together around the fireplace."

Lizzie and ma hurried to finish the household tasks and the cooking so that they could bathe the younger children and then take their own baths before pa and Skip came in from doing the outside work. Lizzie opened the big trunk and took out clean woolen underclothing and clean handknit wool stockings and socks for all the family. She put the garments in neat stacks on ma's bed. Then she brought in the big round tin tub and put it in front of the stove's red eyelets. She watched Frank and

44

George as ma carefully dipped some of the boiling water from the bubbling supply in the iron kettle and cooled it with cold water from the water bucket on the work table. George and Frankie were so little that ma bathed both of them in the same water. But she and Lizzie each used a fresh supply. Lizzie curled cross-legged in the tub as ma soaped her back and time after time squeezed the warm dripping washcloth over the back of her neck. Lizzie's back tingled with the good feel of the swishy soap suds and the clean hot rinse afterward.

They had no sooner dressed, the little boys in starched shirts and woolen trousers, and she and ma in their next to best linsey-woolsey dresses, than pa and Skip tramped in, cold and dirty. Ma hung the dividing curtain across the middle of the dugout after they had carried out the tub and emptied it. Lizzie looked at Skip and thought that one bath water would scarcely be enough for him; he needed at least two soapings and two rinses.

But finally the last tubful was emptied and the dugout set in order. Then the McLeods came down, smiling and cheery-voiced, ready to sit down to the good supper dished up and steaming on the table.

Skip and Lizzie sniffed appreciatively the delicious mingled odors of roast venison, potatoes and gravy, and mince and dried peach pies. They looked greedily at the plates of yellow corn bread made with cracklings and fluffy sourdough biscuits, with their accompanying glasses of wild gooseberry jam and red currant jelly, brought by Mrs. McLeod for the feast. Just when they felt that they would surely starve if they had to wait another minute, pa motioned them to their seats and asked the blessing.

When no one could eat another bite, the men and boys leaned back in their chairs and talked while ma and Mrs. McLeod and Lizzie scraped the plates and stacked the dishes. Ma carefully carried steaming hot water from the big iron kettle on the stove and put some in the dishpan along with a little piece of brown homemade soap. In no time at all the dishes were done and stacked neatly away in the cupboard that pa had made. After that they gathered around the red firelight, pa and ma on straight chairs and Mr. and Mrs. McLeod in the rockers, since they were company. Skip and Lizzie and Frank sat cross legged on the floor, and baby George slept snugly in his trundle bed.

All evening the grown folks talked of Christmases of far away and long ago, when they were little. Skip and Lizzie listened with wide, shining eyes, but tired Frank fell sound asleep, and never knew when ma undressed him and slipped on his warm red flannel nightshirt. And then they sang. Clear and sweet the tones rang out, the deep voices of pa and Mr. McLeod, the treble voices of ma and Mrs. McLeod, and the childish voices of Skip and Lizzie. On and on sang the eager voices, making Christmas out of songs and memories and pioneer courage in the lonely isolation of Rocky Point.

"The sun shines bright in my old Kentucky home;
'Tis summer, the darkies are gay...."

"It came upon a midnight clear,
That glorious song of old,

From angels bending near the earth
To touch their harps of gold...."

"Silent night, holy night,
All is calm, all is bright...."

And then the McLeods were going, with cheerful cries of "Good night and Merry Christmas," while Skip and Lizzie, tired yet excited, took one last look at the row of waiting stockings and tumbled into their beds.

"What's happened to these sleepyheads?" joked pa's deep voice. "Have you forgotten it's Christmas?"

With joyful shouts Skip and Lizzie and Frank jumped out of bed into the welcome warmth of the dugout. There stood pa and ma smiling at them with baby George in ma's arms. And there, hanging from the fireplace mantel, were their four stockings, no longer limp and empty, but full of fascinating bumps and bulges.

"Chwistmas is here," shrieked Frank. "Chwistmas in Frankie's stocking."

With fingers that trembled with eagerness he took the stocking from Lizzie's hands and pulled out its contents of hand-carved toys and sweets. Skip and Lizzie knew just what he would find, for they had helped make some of those very toys, but they could not guess what their own stockings held.

Lizzie's mouth was dry as she unwrapped the bulky parcel stuffed almost the whole length of her long stocking. Skip saw that her eyes blinked fast as she tried to see ahead of the brown wrapping paper, and he saw tears on her lashes as she held the opened gift in her hands and stared down at it.

"O Pa! O Ma!" was all she could say before she began to cry. Her tears fell right down on the face of the beautiful, china-headed doll that pa had brought in the wagon all the way from Canyon City. "It—it's a beautiful doll," she whispered in a choked little voice. "I—I never thought I'd have a doll as nice as this."

Skip thought that Lizzie was too big for dolls, but he didn't say so. He was too busy looking proudly at the new knife that had nestled in the toe of his stocking, along with the shiny red apple and the pieces of hard, store candy.

When Skip saw how pa and ma smiled at their happiness, he could scarcely keep back the eager words that wanted to rush right out and tell ma about the surprise for her Christmas Day. But he knew that he must keep this a secret until the proper time came.

All during the morning hours they played with their gifts. Lizzie dressed and undressed Melinda, the china headed doll, a dozen times. Frank marched his carved animals on long and dangerous journeys across the braided rug and back again, while baby George bit on the fine teething ring that pa had carved. Skip whittled merrily with his knife, admiring anew its keen, shining blades and wondering how he had ever gotten along without it.

Then it was time to go to the McLeods' for Christmas dinner. Again they ate and ate until they could hold no more. And again they settled back for a long visit in the afternoon hours. But this time Skip knew that he was to have some part in the celebration that was to follow.

First there was a surprise for everyone. Pa received a pair of warm woolen mittens that ma had knitted, and Mr. McLeod received a pair of mittens that Mrs. McLeod had knitted. Mr. McLeod had carved two little toy horses for Frank and George, and he gave Skip a big, shining silver dollar, the first that Skip had ever owned. Pa gave ma those yards and yards of lovely calico and grosgrain silk, and pa and ma gave Mrs. McLeod some beautiful brown calico with little white-sprigged flowers scattered all over the smooth surface. Lizzie, hugging Melinda close to her, seemed utterly astonished to find that she was to have another present. Skip couldn't understand her joy over the complete doll wardrobe that Mrs. McLeod and ma had made on the sewing machine that ma had stored in Mrs. McLeod's bedroom.

"I don't see what Lizzie'll do with all that frilly stuff," he said, eyeing the ruffled undergarments and dainty dresses with distaste. "Why, she's as good a runner and wrestler as I am. She'll look downright silly lugging that doll around."

"Sh-h," said Mrs. McLeod in understanding amusement. "Lizzie'll still run and play games with you. But every little girl likes a doll to mother and care for. You're proud of your jackknife, aren't you? Well, that's the way Lizzie feels about her doll."

Skip tried hard to understand, but he still felt that the shining jackknife was a much more important and useful gift than an empty china-headed doll.

"Well, folks," said Mr. McLeod, after the excitement had died down, "I might as well tell you this:

His Voice Sounded Loud in His Own Ears
as He Said, "There, Ma, It's for You."

when good old Father Christmas was here he left somethin' else for one of you. Don't quite know why he chose our house. Said he was leavin' a very special sort of gift."

As soon as Mr. McLeod began talking, Skip saw Mrs. McLeod nod to him. He slipped quietly away to join her in the bedroom. She leaned over and pulled a package from under her bed. "It's all wrapped," she whispered into his ear, her warm breath making a little tickle go shivering down his neck. "I think your mother'll like this better than anything she's ever had."

Skip felt unaccountably shy as he walked out of the bedroom. The sitting room seemed to be much longer than usual and his feet much bigger. He almost stumbled as he put the package on ma's lap, but his voice sounded loud in his own ears as he said, "There, Ma. It's for you."

Skip saw ma's cheeks flush pink as the morning sky as she looked down at the fine rug made from the wolf that Skip had trapped near their dugout roof. It had been nicely tanned by pa and lined with the dark blue material that Mrs. McLeod had saved. But Skip knew what had brought the pink to ma's face and the shine to her eyes.

"Why, Skip, my boy," she said in a tight little voice, and that was all. She bent her head and bit her trembling lips as she gently stroked the soft gray fur. But Skip knew deep in his heart that never again would he give ma any gift that she would treasure as much as she did his wolfskin rug.

Chapter 5
Cabins and Catamounts

IT'S MOVING day. It's moving day," chanted Skip and Lizzie and Frank. They ran excitedly back and forth between dugout and wagon, carrying armloads of clothing and pots and pans. The older children laughed at little George, who toddled after them, echoing "Is Moom Day. Is Moom Day."

"You're getting to be a great big boy, aren't you, honey?" asked Lizzie. She caught his plump little body up in her arms and kissed his rosy cheek. "You're helping sister to get ready to move too. Bless your heart. Come on, Georgie. Sister'll give you something to carry out. Here. Take this kettle."

"I think that's about everything except the dugout itself," joked pa. He expertly packed the last load under the white canvas top and jumped down to shake hands with the McLeods. "Well, folks, guess we'll be on our way. We couldn't fill our old washtub with enough thanks to repay you for all your kindness to us this past winter. So we'll just say again that we want you to come out right often and visit us. We're not so far but what you can see our place from your doorstep."

"That's right," nodded ma smilingly. "Though we hate to leave our good friends, we're really only a mile or so out, right on the edge of the Silvies River. It'll be just a good walk when the roads are dry. We'll be able to see each other often after we get settled in Boone's old log cabin. We are certainly lucky to have it to live in while we're building our new house. The dugout's getting real stuffy these warm spring days."

"It's too bad the Boones moved away," continued ma, motioning to Skip to lift George into the wagon. "But I guess Mr. Boone got discouraged. When he came in to tell us he was leaving he just puckered up his face, shook his head, and said:

"'Snow all day on the second of May
In this country I'll no longer stay.'

"And he hasn't stayed, either. Sometimes it's mighty hard for us pioneering folk to look far enough ahead to see the real worth of a country. It's hard not to get discouraged at times. I know I do."

"We ought to have a good garden this year, Ma," said Lizzie. "Mrs. Boone told me that they raised bucket-sized turnips in their garden patch last year!"

"Oh, they did," Mrs. McLeod added quickly. "I went out, and was astonished at the potatoes, onions, carrots, and parsnips they harvested, besides the turnips. That's good ground out there; make no mistake. We'll be over to see you when your garden's growing, if not before." She smiled teasingly at ma.

"Don't wait for that," laughed pa, helping ma up to the high wagon seat. "There's lots of hard work to be done before then, but McLeod here's the man who's going to help me raise those yellow pine logs after I go up river and float them down. So good-by now, neighbors."

"Good-by, good-by," they all called. Skip, Lizzie, Frank, and George waved and waved as though they were setting out on a journey of hundreds of miles instead of a short one of a mile or two. But they felt as excited and warm inside as though they intended to travel for days.

"It's going to be fun to live in a real log cabin, just as the pioneers did," said Skip. He leaned against the wagon's tailboard and stared back toward the lone house on Rocky Point. "Of course, this isn't a very big place, but pa says that our new cabin will be twenty-four feet long and eighteen feet wide. I guess that'll be big enough for anybody."

"It'll be fun, all right," agreed practical Lizzie. "But don't forget that it'll be hard work, too. You'll have to go with pa to cut those logs and get them in the river. And after they're floated down to the clearing in the willows you'll have to help drag them up out of the water and get them ready for laying. Then when Mr. McLeod comes we'll probably all have to help."

Skip found that Lizzie was right, as usual. After the Whitings were temporarily settled in the Boone cabin, he and pa had plenty to do to keep them busy. First they went fifteen miles upstream, cut the fine yellow pine logs, and floated them down the Silvies River during the spring freshets. Next they harnessed the horses and dragged out the long trees. On these they first used the chopping ax and then the broad ax with its blade eighteen inches wide and slightly crooked handle. They carefully hewed the logs on two sides, inside and out, until they were as smooth as planed lumber.

Skip was glad that pa had come from Maine, where he had run logs. Now pa knew just how to build their new log cabin. When Mr. McLeod came out to help, they got the walls to a height of ten feet, using a chalk line to level the sides. Finally it was done, and they moved once more, this time to their permanent home. The entire family stood back to look thankfully at their handiwork.

First they walked around outside and looked again and again at the long cabin, with its wide front door and open windows with shutters flung back. Proudly the cabin sat in the little clearing in the midst of the huge English willows and river willows and poplars. The good mingled odors of fresh river water, sagebrush, and wild roses perfumed the air and filled them with a keen joy in just being alive on this happy June day of 1875.

Then they all walked inside, ma and pa first, then Lizzie and George, Skip and Frank. There was the big, comfortable sitting room with its huge rock fireplace and, just off to the side, pa and ma's bedroom with little George's trundle bed, and Lizzie's tiny room, each with its homemade slatted bedstead. In the long loft above were the beds for Skip and Frank, and built on the back at the ground-floor level was the snug lean-to with its black iron range, table and chairs, and cupboards. The lean-to was made from real lumber hauled from the little mill at the head of Cow Creek, and its fresh cleanness looked beautiful to eyes tired of dugout rocks and dirt.

"Some of these days we'll have those fine wool mattresses that Mrs. McLeod told me about," said ma, eyeing the straw ticks. "But we'll have to wait awhile before we can make the trip—perhaps until next year."

Busy day followed busy day, with duties for all, even little George. He was not too young to run errands for ma or Lizzie, and all day his small feet trudged willingly back and forth, back and forth. It amused Skip and Lizzie to see his eyes follow the wooden plunger of the five-gallon up-and-down tin churn. He loved to watch as Lizzie sat on the low wooden footbridge near the house, bare feet and cream-filled container in the cooling water, while she churned, churned, churned until her arms ached.

It was on one churning day that Lizzie first heard the sound of horses hoofs. "Pa, Pa, there's a stranger coming," she shouted. She ran to the woodpile, where pa and Skip swung their axes near the growing pile of juniper wood.

"A stranger!" exclaimed pa. He wiped his sweat-beaded face with the back of his forearm as he stopped and straightened his tired back. "Didn't think there were any newcomers in these parts. Reckon we'd better go see."

Skip and Lizzie followed anxiously, close at his heels, as he hurried around the front corner of the log cabin. They smiled with relief as they heard his big voice boom out, "Well, howdy, stranger, and welcome. I reckon from what McLeod's told me that you're Pendleton, the trapper from Emigrant Creek. Am I right?"

"Right as rain," said the stranger, grinning

cheerfully at them. Skip and Lizzie stared curiously at his long hair and beard, and stayed within close range all the rest of the day and evening as they listened to his stories of wild life in the woods and mountains and deserts. So busy was Skip in listening that he ventured not a word until the trapper told of the beaver he had caught. Then the boy could not keep silent.

"You mean you eat them?" he cried, his eyes wide with amazement.

"Only the beaver tails, lad," Pendleton replied. "And a right tasty morsel they be too. First you cut off the tail—that's about a foot and a half long. Then you put a stout stick in the cut end and hold it over the fireplace coals until the scaly covering puffs up. Afterward you peel that off and boil the meat until done; then you put it away to pickle in vinegar. Makes a mighty good morsel for winter eating too. Mighty good."

"But beaver's not the only thing around to watch out for. No, sir. I see signs of catamounts not far from here. Reckon you'd better keep your sights peeled. They're mean customers when they're cornered. I could tell you a thing or two about the ornery critters. They're scared of humans but not of four-footed prey. Caught one after my horse awhile back—catamounts seem to like nothing better than horseflesh. I grabbed my gun and winged him, but he got away. Sure was a big feller. I've been a-lookin' fer him since then, but he's too smart to git caught. I was right glad he didn't get that horse of mine. I'd sure hate to lose Blacky."

Skip leaned forward eagerly to ask another question, but just then ma's quiet voice said, "It's bedtime, children. Run along now. Morning comes early for you sleepyheads."

Much as they longed to stay up, they knew better than to linger after ma had spoken. Skip intended to stay awake and listen to the heavy, rumbling voice downstairs. But somehow his eyes closed for what seemed but a brief moment, and then it was morning, with the tantalizing odor of frying potatoes and onions drifting up into the sun-flooded loft.

It was on this very afternoon that their most exciting adventure since coming to the log cabin took place. Skip found Lizzie down on the footbridge, churning a fresh supply of golden butter.

"Aren't you about done, Liz?" he questioned. "I'd like to go upstream a ways and see if we can locate any cougar tracks. Want to go along?"

"O Skip, I don't think we ought." Lizzie's eyes were round and eager, yet doubtful. "I'd be scared we might see one of those awful catamounts, or whatever they're called. You know what Trapper Pendleton told pa and ma last night about wounding one. Besides, you're supposed to be splitting wood."

Skip impatiently tossed his black hair back from his forehead and moved restlessly, like a young colt chafing for release from a tight rope. "Pa said I didn't have to work this afternoon while he and Pendleton walk in to Rocky Point to see McLeod. Now's our chance to get out and have some fun. Here, I'll help you finish this churning."

His strong young arms grabbed the wooden plunger. Up and down, up and down, it flashed,

58

until the thick clotted cream had turned into a big ball of yellow butter surrounded by delicious golden-flecked buttermilk.

"There," he exclaimed in satisfaction. "Let's carry this up to the house and ask ma if you can't go with me. I'm not going very far."

"It'll be good for you to have a little time free to play," ma answered in reply to Skip's question. "You've both been faithful workers. I'll keep the little boys here. They're out back playing. Don't let them see you leave, or they'll want to go along. Just be sure not to go too far."

"Isn't this fun?" asked Skip, several hours later, from their resting place beneath the shade of a huge English willow tree. They lay on the grassy riverbank near the corral, dangling their hot, tired feet in the cool water. "Whew! I'm plumb tuckered out from running so fast. I had a real good time, though, even if we didn't see any tracks of Pendleton's catamount." He picked up a pebble and idly flipped it, straight and true, to the center of a tree-stump target on the opposite bank.

"I had a much better time *not* seeing any," murmured Lizzie, lying limp as a rag doll on the soft matted grasses. She closed her brown eyes against the sun's slanting rays and wriggled her toes in the soothing, swift-flowing water.

"I don't know what I'd do," thoughtfully mumbled Skip, chewing a sweet-clover stem. "If I'd a gun along I'd have gone farther, but pa said to leave his in the cabin for ma. But if—"

"But if what?" drowsily questioned Lizzie, lulled into half-slumber by Skip's monotone, the buzz of honey-seeking bees, and the little rippling sound of the Silvies River as it swished over the pebbles and rocks near the bordering willows.

"But what?" she repeated, half opening her eyes to see whether Skip was asleep. What she saw jerked her wide awake. She thought wildly that she must be dreaming, for this couldn't be true. It couldn't be!

She turned her head toward Skip, who now sat erect, tense as an arrow poised for flight. His eyes gazed straight up, up into the tall tree nearly overhead. Lizzie drew a short whimpering breath as she again looked toward the great limb that crooked out toward the corral where Mr. Pendleton's horse stamped his feet and whinnied nervously.

They scarcely breathed as they stared at the great, tawny-brown creature crouched on the limb overhead, his long tail swishing restlessly back and forth, back and forth. It was true! Their frightened eyes looked at each other, and again turned in terror toward the overhanging limb.

"Wh—what shall we do, Skip?" Lizzie tried to gulp down the choking lump in her throat. "Skip, we've got to run for our lives."

"Sh—h. Watch, Liz. He isn't after us. He's afraid of people. He's after Pendleton's horse. We've got to save Blacky." Skip spoke bravely, but Lizzie heard his voice tremble.

She wrung her hands in terror and despair. "But you haven't even got a gun. And if we run, he'll come after us. Skip, I'm scared to death."

Lizzie saw Skip's jaws clench together as he shook his head. "Be quiet," he whispered. "I've got

They Scarcely Breathed as They Stared at the Great, Tawny-brown
Creature Crouched on the Limb Overhead

a plan. Here, you can help me. Scoot down a little and pick up some of these rocks. Put them in your apron and bring them to me. There, I've filled my pockets too. Now crawl over here with me—far enough so I can see the cougar's face. When I stand up and start throwing, you run for the house. Get pa's gun and bring it to me. Quick!"

With one swift motion Skip straightened to his feet and threw a small rock directly at the cougar's head. Thud. It landed directly in the snarling cat-amount's face. Blood streamed down beneath its wounded eye, and it half rose, snarling a challenge to the two-legged creature below.

"Run, Liz, run," Skip yelled. Again and again he hurled his ammunition straight into the face of the furious beast. He stood stock still, not daring to move, his heart pounding in his breast. It seemed hours before Lizzie was back, thrusting the gun into his now-empty hands. He dropped to one knee and took careful aim at the blinded beast.

"Boom!" The gun's recoil nearly knocked him over. Blacky plunged wildly and dashed to the opposite side of the small corral. Lizzie burst into excited tears. Ma and little George hurried toward them from the log cabin. Pa and Trapper Pendleton, nearing home, ran with long strides and excited cheers of "Got him, boy. Good shot!"

But Skip, head erect, said nothing. Proudly he walked toward the sprawling, lifeless body of the huge, horse-killing catamount.

Part Two

Other Stories

Already the Raft Was Straining at the Rope, and the Front End
Was Being Pulled Down at a Dangerous Angle

Chapter 6
Rafting on the Amazon

JUST LOOK at that rain, will you?" sighed Cousin Dorothy as she stared sadly out of the window. "I'd hoped the weather would clear up by today, but I guess the weatherman was right when he predicted a near flood sometime this weekend."

"Flood!" scoffed Richard good-naturedly. "You folks up here don't know the meaning of a real flood—the kind that just comes without any warning at all, Amazon fashion. I could tell you a flood story that would make you sit up and take notice."

"Fine," commented Uncle Harvey, who had just come into the living room and settled down for the evening in his easy chair. "We've been hoping that we'd get an exciting story out of you before you went back to the academy. What was this I heard about a flood? We had a mighty bad one last spring not far from here."

"Yes, I remember," nodded Richard soberly. "And it was terrible too. But I was talking about the dreadful sudden floods that come without warning in the tropics. Dad and I were in one that was a regular thriller. I wouldn't want to go through that experience again. It was hair raising." He shuddered at the mere memory of those horror-filled hours, and then looked at his uncle and aunt and cousins. "If you'd really like to hear about it, I'd be glad to tell you," he said, "although I may have forgotten some of the minor details. This happened several years before I came up to the States to go to school."

His audience settled back and looked at him with interest as he began his story:

"I must have been ten or eleven at the time of that January vacation period in Lima. As you'll remember, dad had been transferred back to the Amazon from our former headquarters at Lake Titicaca and La Paz, Bolivia, and we were living at Iquitos. Of course, we had to have a yearly vacation at the coast in order to recover from the jungle climate at the headwaters of the Amazon, and we always looked eagerly forward to the pleasant days at the beach.

"We had to make the round trip by plane, as at that time the road was not completed. So we flew over the high Andes—a five-and-one-half-hour trip. We had a wonderful time at the ocean, and all too soon our vacation ended.

"Dad decided to take back a large number of supplies by boat, because we couldn't afford the high cost of transportation by plane. He had, as I remember, an electric washing machine, several sacks of flour, two five-gallon cans of honey, canned goods, and ten five-gallon cans of kerosene; we couldn't get refined kerosene at Iquitos. In addition to all this we had enough food for ourselves for at least a three-week period, including a large sack of mother's homemade bread, canned beans, tinned butter, and other necessary items.

"Mother, Jack, and Carolyn were to return later by plane, but dad and I started out about five o'clock one morning and traveled all day until we reached the little town where our provisions were waiting for us. These were then loaded on a truck. After this we traveled for several days, first over pavement and then over dirt roads. Our land travel ended at a tiny village on the riverbank, for from that point on the road was impassable in the summer months."

"Summer?" inquired Lillian. "I thought you said it was in January."

"I did," smiled Richard, "but you must remember that in South America the month of January is in our summertime. Well, we stayed at this little village a day or so, sleeping in our own hammocks with collapsible air mattresses, and using mosquito netting to protect our faces. During this time the natives were busy building a big raft from balsa-wood tree trunks. As nearly as I can remember the raft was built of from twenty-five to thirty logs, with the large ends evened off for the front. These buoyant and brittle logs were then tied in about six places with tough jungle vines, and finally crosspieces of a different kind of wood were tied securely on and fastened with short, hard, wooden stakes; No nails were used in the construction.

"At last our heavy load was lashed securely in the little raised and covered platform in the middle of the raft, and we started out on the Aguaytia River, with several native men as guides and oarsmen. At this point the river is shallow and full of rapids, so that great skill is needed in steering. In addition to ourselves and the natives we had as passengers an engineer and a native worker, who also wanted to go to Iquitos.

"Near evening the native oarsmen pulled and tugged at the great one-piece hardwood oars and headed for a sand bar. Dad and I slept on the raft, curled up on the luggage in the thatch-roofed hut, but the others got out their bedding rolls and slept on the sand.

"The next day we went through a narrow gorge, or strait, and this took almost all day. The mountains towered straight overhead, and there was no stopping place anywhere along the jagged shore edges. That same day we had our first real scare. We had just come around a narrow bend when all at once we began to swirl straight toward a rocky island in the middle of the widening channel. In spite of the oarsmen's vigorous efforts the raft continued to head straight for the bar, and would have grounded except for the fact that the men jumped into the shallow water and pushed on the raft with all their might.

"We had just sailed away from this danger point when we almost ran onto a big, wicked-looking snag. In fact, the snag did poke through the cabin floor, and we had visions of hanging there indefinitely, half in and half out of the water. Dad grabbed his hatchet and frantically hacked and cut at the top of the snag until he had broken it off enough to permit the raft to slide free. We all heaved great sighs of relief as we resumed our journey, but then the third misfortune shortly overtook us. This time it wasn't a sand bar or a snag, but worse—it was a log jam, which held us up for some time as we all strained and tugged to free our balsa raft."

As Richard drew a long breath Uncle Harvey leaned forward and spoke earnestly. "I'd say by the time that was over you'd had your share of bad luck for the entire trip. I'd have been ready to give up and return to civilization, I think."

Richard shook his head. "Well, I imagine that dad would have appreciated the sight of civilization about that time. But there we were, with all our provisions, and there was nothing left to do but go ahead. We couldn't go back. By that time it was getting late on Friday afternoon, and we looked for a place to tie up in the deep, narrow gorge, although dad hated to stay there all night. But it would be far too dangerous to travel after dark, as we might strike rocks or logs and sink our raft.

"Late in the afternoon we came to a point where the river was very low. There we sighted a sand bar about five feet wide lying at the bottom of a moderate slope. Dad said that we'd better tie the raft to an enormous water soaked log at the edge of the sand, so the oarsmen swung in there and fastened the tie rope securely. No sooner had they done so than a number of ferocious looking wild boars charged down out of the jungle to drink at the river. I shivered with fright as the men hastily grabbed their guns, in case the beasts should attack us, but I guess they were more afraid of us than we were of them. At any rate, they stampeded back up the slope, and I was more than glad to see them vanish, I can tell you.

"The men pitched camp; then we ate. Afterward dad and I piled more of our goods around the edge of our shelter just in case any more wild animals should investigate our boat. Then we went to bed, tired out after our long and exciting day.

"I don't know just what time we woke up, but it was sometime in the middle of the night. When we opened our eyes we heard the rain pouring down and the men shouting at one another. They were out in the downpour, waving their flashlights toward the river. I jumped out of bed to find that I was wading ankle deep in water, for the current had risen so swiftly that by now the leaves of the jungle trees high up on the top of the slope were directly over the top of our raft roof. In only a few hours the river had risen ten or fifteen feet. Already the raft was straining and tugging at the rope fastened to the big log, and the front end of our boat was being pulled down at a dangerous angle into the muddy water.

"'We'll have to sacrifice some of our load,' dad said. 'If we don't, we'll lose everything we have.' It was hard to decide what to toss overboard, but finally he chose two sacks of our precious flour. Although he didn't tell us until afterward, he was afraid that we'd all drown in the raging torrent. By now it was a terrible, seething mass of muddy water, and it rolled by us with the thundering noise of an express train.

"Every once in a while we could hear wild, despairing shouts as some unfortunate travelers were whirled downstream, some to be cast up on shores far, far below us, and some to vanish forever from sight. Even now it makes my blood run cold as I recall those hoarse voices screaming, 'O hermanos, *salvenos que nos aogamos! Ayuda! Ayuda!'* (O brethren, save us else we drown! Help! Help!)

"In the midst of our terror and despair dad knelt down right there in the pouring rain and prayed aloud in his deep, earnest voice, asking God to help us and to spare our lives and the lives of all those in danger from the flood. The sound of his calm voice was a comfort to all of us, for the men were almost as frightened as I.

"I'll never forget those texts that dad quoted either. I may forget many things, but those texts will always be a part of me:

"'God is our refuge and strength, a very present help in trouble. Therefore will not we fear, though the earth be removed, and though the mountains be carried into the midst of the sea; though the waters thereof roar and be troubled, though the mountains shake with the swelling thereof.' 'Be still, and know that I am God. The Lord of hosts is with us; the God of Jacob is our refuge.' Psalms 46:1-3, 10, 11.

"'When thou passeth through the waters, I will be with thee; and through the rivers, they shall not overflow thee.' Isaiah 43:2.

"We thought that Sabbath morning would never come, but when at last it was daylight we almost wished for night, for now we could see the desolate, rain-soaked landscape around us. We could scarcely believe our eyes when we found our raft perched up on the top of the little slope that last night lay so far above us. Dad told me to grab my good shoes and hurriedly crawl out on a nearby tree limb. I did just as he said, edging carefully along the slippery wood and sliding down the tree trunk into the water around the base. All at once I got so excited that I put my new shoes down, and I never did find them after that.

"Three of the natives stayed with the raft while one man slashed his way back into the jungle with a machete and got some vines that he first tied to a tree farther back in the dense jungle and then to the front end of the raft. All this time our makeshift boat had been straining hard at the rope, until by now it was tipped at a dangerous angle, pointing down toward the old log. Dad was desperately afraid we'd lose the washer that mother had wanted for such a long time, as well as our other precious provisions, so we hurried to cut the rope that had been tied the evening before. As soon as the sharp knife severed the rope strands, the raft shot a foot or so out of the water before settling back on the flood crest.

"All day Sabbath the men kept trying to pull the raft back from the high, turbulent waters that raged past, for great logs hurtled downstream, often missing us by mere inches. Several of the men built a temporary shelter on the highest point of land available, using poles and a thatch somewhat like palm leaves for a roof. Then they kindled a big fire, where we tried to warm ourselves and dry out, at least partially, for all this time the rain was falling in regular torrents, and for hours we had been soaked to the skin.

"While the men were struggling to save the raft, I went a short distance from our makeshift camp to try to find a spring, so that we could get fresh drinking water. I walked slowly and carefully, too, you may be sure, for I'd made several trips on the

Amazon in the mission launch when dad went out on his missionary trips, and I knew that it didn't pay to take any chances. You'd scarcely believe how many wild creatures I saw small deer licking at the water trickling from rocks, snakes lying in the trees or on the ground, monkeys the size of your cocker spaniel, green parrots—but all of them were evidently too wet and miserable to bother about me, and I didn't waste any time with them. There were other animals near by, too. At night we saw fierce eyes gleaming on the outer edge of the camp-fire, and knew that wild boars and panthers lurked in the outer ring of darkness around our flickering firelight.

"The flood water kept rising until about the middle of Sabbath afternoon, for every two hours we measured from the stake at the water's edge. On Sunday morning we woke to find that our raft, instead of being afloat on the fifteen-foot crest of the flood, was now stranded on the top of the earth slope. It was the queerest feeling imaginable to look down over the edge of our raft down, down, to the river many feet below us. The waters had dropped as rapidly as the torrential cloudburst had caused them to rise, and we were left in the treetops instead of the river.

"I won't take the time to describe the almost impossible task of unloading our provisions and trying to push the raft loose. After much hard work the men succeeded in cutting the raft in two, prying and sliding each half down the bank into the river and finally tying on new crosspieces with the ever-present stout jungle vines. It takes but a few minutes to tell it, but it took all day Sunday and until 3 P.M. Monday to accomplish this and reload the various articles. We were tired and we were hungry, for the natives' food had been washed away, and we had shared our provisions with them. Even if we'd had plenty to eat, we couldn't have had any hot food, for by now the matches and wood were water soaked.

"By this time dad was suffering with a severe attack of malaria, and we didn't know what to do. Even our medicine box had been washed away. When we at length sailed out of that dreadful gorge we found that even out in the flat country beyond, the water had risen to a depth of five feet. We stopped at a village, where we found an old woman who had a few quinine pills left. These she generously let dad take upon his solemn promise to send back to her a double amount—a promise he kept as soon as he reached civilization.

"On Monday night we camped at a deserted Indian *chacra* (farm), where we found a few half-ripened papayas and a small bunch of half-eaten bananas that the parrots had left on the trees. This food may not sound very appetizing to you, but to us it tasted delicious.

"Tuesday we went on down the river and came to another Indian village, where we secured some coals for our cooking fire on the raft and five fifty-pound sacks of huge oranges the size of American grapefruit. For all this fruit we paid somewhere around 65 cents American money.

"After this we traveled all night, because the river was very wide from this point on to the mouth

74

of the Ucayali. Often men with motorboats came hurrying out from the shore to ask for word of other missing travelers. It was then that we learned that many people had been lost, and that one man had lost a small fortune in expensive machinery.

"At last we came to our destination, where we found a hotel and comfortable beds. Here we stayed for three days, recuperating from our dangerous raft trip and waiting for the big steamer that would carry us the five-day journey on to Iquitos, our home, where mother, Jack, and Carolyn were waiting anxiously for us.

"So," Richard said, smiling at his eager listeners, "you can understand that whenever I look out at a heavy rainfall in this country I'm reminded of our terrifying experience in a South American cloudburst. And I'm thankful to be right here instead of down in that gorge, struggling to save not only our raft but also our lives."

As in a Dream She Heard Her Classmates Shout, "Go On, Gwendolen"

Chapter 7
Cecil's Hill Crash

B UT YOU promised, Mother," wailed Gwendolen. Hot tears filled her eyes as she rubbed the frosted windowpane and stared blindly out across the snow-filled valley.

"You promised that I could go coasting on Cecil's Hill with Hal and Hazel, and I've been counting on it for days and days. Next week we'll have to go back to school, and then there won't be any time for play—hardly any, at least."

"Yes, dear, I know," sighed mother patiently. "I really did promise that you could go to Cecil's Hill with the Hibbard children, but that was before you were ill in bed with a severe cold. Sometimes it is best not to hold one to a promise when circumstances have changed previously made plans."

"But I'm well enough now," teased Gwendolen. "After all, I've been up and around the house since Monday, and I feel just fine. O Mother, I can hardly wait to try out the new sled that grandpa gave me. Please, please let me go."

Mrs. Lampshire put her arm around her daughter and kissed the soft young cheek, looking at her intently before she spoke.

"Since you are almost well, and since I did promise, I am going to let you go—"

"O Mother, thank you. Thank you!" interrupted Gwendolen, twirling round and round in her excitement, her wool dress flaring out over her black stockinged legs.

"Just a moment, dear," mother added. "I hadn't quite finished. It is because you have been an obedient girl that I am giving you permission, and there are two requests that I am going to ask you to obey. The first is that you must not be gone longer than one hour, and the second is that you must not take more than two long slides down Cecil's Hill road.

"The air is very cold, even though the sun is shining, and as an onlooker you are likely soon to be chilled through. Besides this, Mrs. Hibbard told me today that the hill is very icy. All the neighborhood children have been carrying buckets of water from the pump in Mr. Cecil's yard and pouring it on the sidewalk. By now the water has frozen into a solid sheet of ice. Your new sled with its sharp runners will travel like lightning. I know that you are not yet strong enough to steer it safely past the telephone pole at the bottom of the steep sidewalk runway. Be sure to stay out in the middle of the main road, away from the narrow footpath. You'll find the road itself quite smooth enough for good coasting."

"Hello! We're ready," called Hazel from the big bare poplar tree by the front gate. As soon as Gwendolen opened the door she continued, her breath rising like a white cloud in the bitterly cold air, "Hal's coming in just a minute and then we're going around the block to get Burns McGowan and Frances and Teresa. Next we'll go past Dr. Geary's and get Woodbridge too.

"Be sure to wrap up good and warm. It's awfully cold. I'll go on over to Donegan's, and you can come along with Hal." She beat her mittened hands together before she hurried down the snow-encrusted walk, her old homemade sled dragging at her heels.

Gwendolen hurried into her warm winter coat as she heard Hal's shrill whistle. She fastened the heavy black galoshes and pulled on her red hand-knit tassel cap and mittens. Then she gave her mother a hasty kiss, grabbed the new sled at the edge of the steps, and, with Hal, hurried toward the group of children waiting impatiently at the corner.

"Oh, good!" cried Hazel. "I was really afraid that your mother'd make you stay at home today. We wouldn't have had nearly so much fun without you." Hazel's sky-blue eyes flashed joyfully as she spied the new red-and-yellow sled.

"Look at that beautiful red Flyer! Aren't you a lucky girl, though! I can barely wait to see how fast it'll go. I'm anxious to see you try it on the icy footpath on Cecil's Hill. You'll be sure to win over everyone else."

"You've got to win," nodded Teresa. "We've planned a race with the eighth graders, and our seventh grade has just *got* to win."

"I—I guess I could win, all right." Gwendolen's heart sank as she saw her playmates' eager faces looking directly at her. "But—well, you see, mother doesn't want me to go down the footpath today. She says it's dangerous when covered with so much ice. She's afraid that I might have an accident."

"Oh, pooh!" scoffed Burns, tossing his red head defiantly. "There's ab-so-lutely nothing to be afraid of. Ab-so-lutely nothing. Why, there's a high stone wall all along one side, so you couldn't slide off the path if you wanted to. And any sissy could steer clear of that pole at the bottom. You can see it ahead of you for two blocks before you get there."

He stopped and eyed her curiously before he continued. "Besides, you've gone down that path hundreds of times and nothing's ever happened to you. Don't tell me you're getting to be a fraidy cat." He shrugged his plump shoulders and eyed her scornfully.

Gwendolen's cheeks burned and her throat ached with the unkind words that she longed to answer. But instead she trudged along in silence as her playmates hurried ahead to the top of the hill.

"Hurry up, everybody. We're almost ready to start."

Happy greetings and gay laughter filled the wintry air as several dozen schoolmates gathered in an excited huddle to plan the order of racing. Gwendolen stood on the outside of the circle, where she could get a closer look at the long, steep slope of the narrow, frozen footpath. How smooth and glassy it looked with its clear ice crust gleaming in the sunlight. Sharp little tingles ran up and down her spine as she imagined the wonderful feel of the rushing wind on that swooping plunge and the breath-taking coldness of the spraying ice crystals as they blew across her bare face.

She stood there, thinking how she would love to coast down that steep slope!

She cast a disdainful glance at the wide road beyond. Flying figures on gaily painted sleds darted like swallows down its hard,packed snow and toiled antlike up its steep slope. Gwendolen thought that it might be fun to coast there *if* the forbidden footpath were not so temptingly near.

"Come on. Let's go down, just for practice, before the races begin," called a voice right in her ear. She jumped as she turned around and looked into Frances' cheerful, rosy face.

"I can't go down the path today," she said slowly. "And mother told me not to go down the road more than two times. She's afraid I'm still rather weak after being in bed so long."

"You look all right to me," Frances answered, looking critically at her friend. "You've got just as many freckles as ever, although they do look a little paler. Well, it's too bad, but it can't be helped. Your mother always means just what she says, and if you disobey, I know you won't be allowed to coast for ever so long. But it is a shame! Those old eighth graders are sure to win if you don't help our side, and they'll never let us forget it, either. We'd counted on your new sled today." She sighed as she walked slowly toward June and Mildred.

Gwendolen's heart sank with disappointment. So bitter were her angry thoughts that she scarcely heard the loud, excited cries of "Go. Hurry. Faster.

Rah! Rah! Rah! for the eighth grade," as, one by one, the older students flew like snowbirds downward to victory, finishing a few inches ahead of the out-distanced seventh graders.

The creeping cold and her classmates' cries for revenge startled her into action. "I might as well take my first turn," she thought, "before I get too cold to move. My hour must be nearly up, so I might as well have a little fun while I can."

She pulled her sled over to the top of the roadway and, lying flat along its shiny untried surface, started down, side by side with Regina, one of the eighth-grade contestants.

"Rah! Rah! Rah! for our side. Three cheers! We won," shouted the joyous seventh-grade onlookers from the hilltop, gleefully dancing up and down.

"Good for you, Gwendolen. Try it again. Maybe we've still got a chance to win," Burns shouted loudly through his cupped hands.

"9 to 6. Isn't that the score?" asked Woodbridge anxiously as he shivered in the sharp December wind. "Oh, if we could only make four points we'd be ahead."

"That's right, we would," added Hal. "And think how much fun it would be to go back to school as the Cecil's Hill winners. We'd show those smart eighth graders that we can outrace them. But it looks pretty hopeless right now."

As Gwendolen pulled her Flyer to the very top of the hill her excited companions rushed toward her and urged her to race again. Without stopping to think about the unaccustomed pounding in her chest or the unusual shortness of her breath, she again flung herself upon the beautiful new coaster. Three more times she swept down the hill to victory, and three more times she climbed the hill with her friends' cries ringing sweetly in her hum-ming ears. But now her knees wobbled slightly, and she gratefully sank down on the sled's smooth surface to rest.

"We're winning. We're winning," cried Hazel. "You beat Frank Loggan last time, and now it's a tie. 9 to 9. O Gwendolen, you've got to go once more. You can do better than any of us, and we've just *got* to win."

"Come on," yelled Hal. "We've decided to run the last race on the footpath. It's wide enough for two sleds and it's as slick as glass. This race'll really be exciting."

Gwendolen had felt pleasantly warmed by her classmates' praise and by the excitement of the race. She jumped quickly to her feet only to stop short. For the very first time since entering the contest she remembered her mother's warning. "I want you to take only two slides down the hill. Stay out in the middle of the main road. I know that you're not strong enough yet to steer your sled down the narrow footpath."

Suddenly the warm, pleasant glow left her, and she felt pale and cold. She half opened her lips to say, "But I can't coast on the footpath. I promised mother that I wouldn't. And I've already coasted down more times than I'm allowed to do today."

But somehow the words stuck in her throat, and try as she might she could not say them. Mutely she pulled her Flyer over to the top of the footpath and waited for her opponent to reach the starting line. As in a dream she heard her classmates shout, "Go on, Gwendolen. You've got to win. You've just got to!" As in a dream she heard the eighth grade cheer wildly for Frank Loggan.

Then without stopping to listen further to that disturbing little inner voice Gwendolen flung herself upon her sled. She stared straight ahead as the steel runners began to bite sharply into the sparkling surface. How narrow and steep the path suddenly became. She shook her dizzy head as the Flyer gathered momentum and sped faster and faster beside the high stone fence. She stared anxiously ahead, blinking her dazzled eyes in a vain attempt to banish the black specks that floated strangely in front of her. Swallowlike she swooped down over the sparkling crystals, her sled runners cutting crisply along the dangerous, glassy path.

Closer and closer and closer she rushed toward the huge telephone pole at the end of the runway. It loomed larger and larger before her frightened eyes. Her heart leaped as the object seemed to move directly into her pathway. Gwendolen's mittened hands tried frantically to tighten their grasp upon the steering bar, but all her efforts were in vain. Her arms felt cold and limp and lifeless as her hands clung numbly to the now unguided sled careening wildly out of control.

Thirty feet, twenty feet, ten feet—then with a sickening thud she crashed head-on into the immovable telephone pole at the foot of Cecil's Hill.

Gwendolen felt one sharp blow before she sank down, down into a thick, smothering blackness that rolled up and around her until the sun and daylight were completely blotted out and she knew nothing more.

A hoarse rasping noise that intermingled strangely with frightened voices sounded in Gwendolen's ears as she struggled back to consciousness. But it was several moments before she realized that the rough noise was her own painful, labored breathing. She tried to move, only to wince in pain at the slight effort.

"Here. Don't move. We'll lift you onto my sled and pull you home," Hazel said sympathetically as she knelt down and rubbed Gwendolen's forehead with a handful of snow.

"Oooooooh! Ouch!" moaned the unfortunate victim. "Wh-what—"

"Don't try to talk," warned Hal. "You crashed head-on into the big telephone pole, and it knocked you breathless. You've got a bump the size of a goose egg on your head and a cut on your arm, but I really don't think any bones are broken. We'll hurry and get you home, though, if you think you can stand being moved. I expect your mother'll want to call Dr. Geary."

Gwendolen never forgot the agony of that bumpy, jolting ride over the ridges of hard-frozen snow in the rutted road. Every jar sent a sharp, knifelike pain through her bruised head and bleeding arm. And the sight of Burns carrying the sad remaining sticks of her once-beautiful new Flyer was almost more than she could bear.

It seemed an hour before the sad little procession turned in at the front gate to be met by white-faced Mrs. Lampshire. It seemed another hour before she was at last tucked safely into her warm, comfortable bed, with mother hovering sympathetically near while kind Dr. Geary looked at her bandaged arm and gave her a sedative. She was just drifting off to sleep when she heard the doctor speak to mother.

"Well, from what Woodbridge told me, I guess this girl of yours won the Cecil's Hill coasting championship for the seventh grade. He said that she was a full sled length ahead in crossing the goal line just before she crashed. Too bad the new sled's ruined, though. Her injuries will soon heal, but that sled's damaged beyond repair. I took a look at it as I came in, and there's nothing left but kindling wood."

Gwendolen's heavy eyes opened slowly and looked waveringly into mother's sorrowful face. Though her tongue felt strangely thick and it was an effort to talk, she felt that she must speak to mother.

"It—it served me right, Mother," she whispered shakily. "You knew best after all! I just wasn't strong enough to steer away from danger, and I deserved my punishment. Winning that contest for the seventh grade wasn't at all important compared to disobeying you and ruining my beautiful sled. Next time I'll know better than to hold you to a promise."

Chapter 8
The "Evil Eye"

JENNIFER TURNED quickly as her mother entered the comfortable living room, her full blue skirt swirling about her slim young figure. "I don't care," she stormed. "Lynn Foster just doesn't belong, that's all, and that's exactly why I didn't mail her invitation along with all the others. I don't like her, and neither does anyone else in our school crowd. I'm sorry if I sound rude, Mother, but nothing you say can make me change my mind. That's the way we all feel. If you make us invite her, it'll simply ruin the party for everyone. Won't it, Jack?"

Sixteen-year-old Jennifer's green eyes almost flashed fire as she turned toward her twin brother for the loyal support that he always gave.

"Jen's right, Mother," Jack nodded slowly. "I hate to make unkind remarks about any girl, but sis really's got the right slant. Oh, it isn't that there's anything actually wrong with Lynn, and she's an awfully good student. In fact, she gets straight A's. But—well, she's what you'd call a complete washout—no pep, no personality, no nothing. She's been invited to lots of things, but she always refuses. And she's never invited any of us to her home."

"Sit down, youngsters," said mother sympathetically. "Now, suppose you start at the beginning and tell me what's wrong. I'm afraid that I can't judge very fairly when hearing only one side of the story."

Jack nodded knowingly to his sister. "That's mother for you, Jen, every single time. You might know that you won't get any sympathy until she hears Lynn's side of the story too. And maybe you won't get any sympathy even then. It's always hard to guess what mother's going to decide. But one thing sure, it'll be right, no matter what it is, or how hard for us to take."

Jennifer sighed in exasperation as she retorted, "All right, Jack, but I still say that Lynn doesn't belong, even though she's lived here for over a year.

"And it isn't because she hasn't pretty clothes, Mother. Or it isn't because she and her grandparents sell milk and eggs, and bring them in from that little farm on the edge of town. You know that none of our crowd's the least bit snobbish. We wouldn't care if she had to wear gunny sacking if she'd only join our activities and be a part of the bunch.

"Honestly, we've asked her to be in class assembly programs; our music teacher wanted her to join the glee club; and Mr. Blane invited her to be a member of the debating team. But she just sticks her nose up in the air and says, 'No, thank you,' to everything. Why, she even refused to go to our Spanish Club party at Sally's house. Really, Mother, if we lived in the Pilgrim period that we're studying in history class, I'd say she had an 'Evil

If We Live in the Pilgrim Period That We're Studying in History Class,
I'd Say She Had an "Evil Eye"

Eye,' because she simply ruins everybody's good time by the way she stares at us."

"Well, suppose we wait until daddy's home tonight. Then we'll decide what to do about the party," mother counseled. "I'm going to drive out to see her grandmother. I should have gone long before now. She may be really ill. Hurry along so that you'll be through with your work when I return. We've much planning to do before Saturday night, you know."

It was evening before the entire family gathered around the blazing fireplace logs. Daddy sat in his favorite armchair, mother in her rocker, the twins on the settee, and nine-year-old Jimmie sprawled on the bear-skin rug in front of the hearth.

"This October air's certainly crisp," daddy said as he held his cold hands toward the welcome warmth of the fireplace. "A crackling fire feels good. I just stepped out on the porch for a look at the night sky. The moon's beautiful. It'll be as light as day for your Saturday evening party, twins."

At mention of the party Jennifer's face brightened, until mother looked up quickly and said, "That reminds me, dear. I saw Lynn's grandmother today. She hasn't been well, but she was up and around in the house when I arrived, fretting that she couldn't do more to help Lynn. She asked about the party—"

"Mother!" Jennifer exclaimed. "You didn't tell her about it, did you? Oh, dear, now Lynn'll be sure to come. She'll wear one of her plain, dark school dresses and sit around and stare and—and—"

"And cast an 'Evil Eye' on us?" sympathized Jack.

"Exactly! And the first thing you know, our

party'll be ruined—just ruined." Tears of self-pity sprang into Jennifer's pretty eyes.

"Perhaps she's only timid or bashful, instead of critical," mother suggested.

"Timid!" scoffed Jennifer. "Bashful! I don't think there's anything timid or bashful about her. No, she just wants to act hateful and spoil our fun."

But mother shook her head as she put down her crocheting, and reached toward a large red and gold volume on the reading table at her elbow.

"No, I don't agree with you. Often young people—and older people as well—act very distant and proud when they're really longing to make friends. Sometimes they may actually seem rude, but I'm sure that if we could only find the right keys to unlock their lonely hearts, we'd discover many new, loyal friends."

"By the way," mother continued, "you spoke jokingly of the 'Evil Eye' today. You've asked Edwin to your party, haven't you?"

"Why, of course," hastily nodded Jack. "We wouldn't have much fun without Edwin. He's more fun than all the rest of us put together. But what in the world has his invitation to do with witchcraft?" His puzzled eyes sought Jennifer's but found no answer there.

Mother smiled as she opened the thick book. She looked at the twins and at Jimmie before she turned the pages to several marked passages. "I wondered if you'd invite him if you knew that one of his ancestors was accused of casting an 'Evil Eye' upon several of the villagers of Northampton, away back in the year 1656?" she began.

"What?" chorused three young voices, as six amazed eyes looked straight at her. "Do you mean that one of Edwin's ancestors was accused of being a witch?" gasped Jennifer.

"That's correct," nodded mother. "After our talk today I thought that you might be interested in this true story of what really happened to the ancestor of one of our neighborhood families. Would you like to hear this early day happening? I came across it while doing some research for our Library Club."

"Would we! Of course we would. Go ahead, please, Mother," Jennifer urged. The three young people settled back ready to listen.

"Very well," said mother, "but I think I'll tell you the story in my own words rather than read directly from Henry Parson's *History of the Parsons Family*, a book formerly owned by Edwin's grandmother. Mr. Parsons has used some of the witchcraft account in Trumbull's *History of Northampton*, but I believe that it'll be easier for Jimmie to understand if this story is told rather than read.

"I hope that you'll listen closely, for to us today it seems almost impossible that any intelligent person could believe that a neighbor had sold her soul to the devil in return for a part of his evil power.

"Our story begins in that period of history that you are now studying, and concerns the Pilgrims, who came over in the *Mayflower* or shortly afterward. One of these was Joseph Parsons, from Devonshire, England, who became the chief founder of Northampton, Massachusetts. He was a man of considerable wealth and importance. The other was Mary Bliss, who also was born in Devonshire,

England, in 1620. She came to the Connecticut Valley with her parents, and in 1646 she was married to Joseph Parsons.

"For a time they lived at Springfield, where they had among their neighbors a family by the name of Bridgman. We are not told what caused a 'falling out' among these friends, but something serious must have happened, for Sarah Bridgman turned against Mary Parsons, whispering to other neighbors that if they valued their lives, they should stay away from Mary. She said that in her opinion Mary had been given certain evil powers by the devil and that she had the satanic gift of the Evil Eye.

"Some time before 1656, when Mary was about thirty years old, the Parsons had moved to Northampton. They were soon followed by several Springfield families, including the Bridgmans. Sarah Bridgman lost no time in telling her new Northampton neighbors the same witchcraft stories about Mary Parsons that she had told her former Springfield neighbors.

"Although many people complained that Mary was very proud, she was really most tenderhearted. Of course, these falsehoods wounded her deeply, for she was an honest Christian woman. When her mother visited her Mary cried and told her about the gossip. Mary's mother immediately went to see Sarah. She told Sarah that she had been telling very serious falsehoods about Mary, and that Joseph Parsons could not overlook such an insult to his wife.

"Sarah said she knew that Mary was a witch, and that she would not take back her words, for Mary had bewitched some of their fine farm animals and had caused them to die. Later on, Sarah became even more bitter, and said that Mary's witchcraft had caused the death of her own little child.

"Then Sarah's eleven-year-old son fractured his knee. It was very poorly set by the doctor, and the little fellow in his agony cried out that Mary Parsons was pulling his leg off, and that he saw her on the shelf. He said that when she went away from the shelf a black mouse followed her. In those days people believed that a person who was a witch could change herself at will into the form of any animal, and thus escape capture."

"But, Mother, that couldn't possibly be true," cried wide-eyed Jimmie, now sitting cross-legged on the rug.

"Why, no one could believe such nonsense!"

"Oh, but they did," said mother. "Another neighbor, William Hannum, quarreled with Mary about the use of her brother John's oxen. Soon afterward a strange disease killed a 'lusty cow' and a 'lusty swine' that had before this been well and healthy. A day or so after their disagreement William traveled to Windsor with his cart and oxen. While on the way, one of the cattle was bitten by a rattlesnake and died right there in the road. Of course, he blamed Mary for all his bad luck, saying that she was one of the devil's witches."

"You can see, Jimmie," added daddy, "that those folk had made up their minds to believe one certain fact. They wouldn't reason. They were just plain stubborn. It's a good thing that none of us today are stubborn in our beliefs." Jennifer flushed but remained silent as she saw the sly twinkle in her father's eyes.

"Well," continued mother, "a Mrs. Hannum also added her voice to the gossip. She said that many people had warned her to stay away from Mary Parsons. Then she said that Mrs. Parsons had tried to hire her daughter, probably as a housemaid, asking her to live at the Parsons home. But Mrs. Hannum had said no and, following her refusal, the daughter sulked and refused to help with her home duties. Mrs. Hannum was afraid that her daughter had had an evil spell cast over her. But the truth of the matter was that the daughter was sulking because she was not allowed to go and live with the wealthiest family in town. Daughters of the seventeenth century were not one bit different from twentieth-century daughters.

"At last Joseph Parsons brought charges of slanderous gossip against Sarah Bridgman, saying that Sarah had falsely accused Mary, his beloved wife, of being a witch. To that community, in those days of belief in witchcraft, this was a very serious thing. People firmly believed that Satan received the soul of a witch as payment for the gift of his evil power. They also believed that the witches could ride through the air to one of their meeting places and there hold what was fearfully called a Witches Sabbath—just the opposite of the blessed true Sabbath of the Lord. Naturally Joseph could not tolerate the statement that his good wife belonged to one of these unholy groups.

"The court solemnly stated that Mary was not a witch, and Sarah was ordered to confess her mistake and to pay a fine to the Parsons family."

"That was certainly a lucky ending!" exclaimed Jack. "Mrs. Parsons must have been glad when the trial was over and she could go back home."

"Unfortunately poor Mary's sorrows hadn't ended with her trial for witchcraft," mother stated gravely. "You'll learn that an ugly, critical attitude is hard to kill. It often lives on for years, whereas the good that people do is forgotten. Here is the second half of Mary Parsons' story.

"Eighteen long years passed. I suppose that they were busy, happy ones, for Mary was the mother of a family of thirteen children. When her youngest child was only two years old, a married daughter of the same Bridgman family that had caused her so much sorrow died in Northampton. This daughter's illness was not understood by the local doctor, and immediately the cry of 'witch, witch,' was directed toward Mary. This time the trial was held in Boston, where Mary appeared before the court and bravely pleaded her own case. She swore that she was innocent of such awful crimes, but the jury refused to listen to her. This poor woman was imprisoned for two months before her trial was held. A jury of good women were chosen 'to make a diligent search of the body of Mary Parsons, whether any marks of witchcraft appear.' They reported their findings, but we are not told what they were."

"What were the marks of witchcraft, Mother?" questioned Jimmie. "How could they tell anything just by looking at her?"

"I'm not sure, Jimmie. I haven't been able to find too much about the witchcraft marks. But I have read that a witch was supposed to have on her body certain spots where no pain could be felt. These pain free spots were places where the devil had touched the witch. If these marks were pricked with a sharp instrument, and the victim showed no pain, she was immediately put to death, for this test proved her to be one who had become a servant of Satan. Another test was the trial by water, in which the poor victim was thrown into the river. If she floated, she was a witch. If she sank, she was innocent. In either case she lost her life!

"This jury also declared that Mary was not a witch, and she was set free. Again she returned to her home, where she lived to the ripe old age of ninety-two, dying in 1712, twenty-seven years after the death of her loyal husband.

"Although Mary was never again charged with the sin of witchcraft, she lived through those

If She Floated, She Was a Witch.
If She Sank, She Was Innocent.

dreadful trials, persecutions, and punishments for witchcraft that took place in Massachusetts in 1692, just eighteen years after her second trial. In the spring of that year a wave of hysterical excitement swept over New England, and between May and September of that year several hundred persons were arrested. Thirty-two persons were put to death in these trials. Of this number nineteen were hanged and one was pressed to death under a heavy weight. Happily, by October of the same year, people began to regain their right senses. Early in the following year all those in prison were freed, even though they had never been put on trial."

"Well, can you imagine people acting like that!" Jimmie burst forth. "I'm glad that people today aren't so stupid. Imagine anyone thinking that a woman with thirteen children could be a witch!"

There was silence as mother closed the book and laid it on the table. No one else said a word until Jennifer cleared her throat. "I—I guess I'm not too stupid to see the point," she said slowly. "Of course I know that Lynn's not rich or prominent or a leader in the community but—"

"But she could be a leader if she had a chance," broke in Jack excitedly. "Isn't that what you meant, Mother? Didn't you mean that Lynn hasn't had a fair chance here? Maybe we're the ones who turned our school friends against her in the first place—just like that Mrs. Bridgman did with Mary Parsons."

Mother's warm smile shone on the twins and Jimmie as she answered. "I'll tell you what I learned today when I visited Lynn's grandmother. Then you can make your own decision. Lynn's grandfather has been so crippled by rheumatism that he is scarcely able to do any work. Lynn has been milking four cows night and morning, helping care for the large flock of chickens, and trying to deliver the milk and eggs to town customers. She also helps with the housework as much as possible. She has a strong sense of loyalty to her grandparents. They have cared for her since her parents were killed in a train wreck ten years ago. Lynn has done all this for some weeks and kept up her schoolwork as well. I don't wonder that she seems tired and listless.

"However, I don't think you'll need to worry about having Lynn at your party Saturday night," mother slyly concluded. "Her grandmother told me that Lynn wouldn't be able to come. She has no party clothes, and they cannot buy any."

"Indeed she is coming," said Jennifer, her green eyes full of tears, and her soft red lips trembling with shame and remorse. "She's coming right to this house tomorrow. I'm going to look over the clothing that Cousin Sally just sent. I'm sure there'll be something that Lynn can wear. Why, of course. That flame-and-gold party dress would do wonders for her. You'll help us if there's much sewing to do, won't you, mother?"

"I certainly will," said mother happily as she and daddy looked understandingly at each other. "But now it's nearly bedtime. Let's have our Bible study; then we'll be off to sweet dreams."

Jennifer was right. The flame-and-gold party dress was beautiful on shy little Lynn. Under its magic spell she blossomed into a gypsylike beauty of her own that quite surprised Jennifer. Busily they fitted not only Cousin Sally's discarded party dress but also several good-as-new wool suits and a cunning red plaid dress. What fun the girls had as they chattered and laughed in Jennifer's dainty pink-and-white bedroom. As Jennifer brushed and curled Lynn's soft, black hair she was astonished to find how much fun she was having.

"I've had such a good time," Lynn said as she at last turned to leave the room. She threw her arms around Jennifer and gave her a quick, shy kiss. "I can't thank you enough for all you and your mother have done," she said warmly. "You know, I always thought you were so distant and cold. You seemed to be making fun of me, and so did all the rest of our class. But I guess I was to blame. I wanted to be friendly, but I was afraid you'd laugh at me if I joined the activities. I've never had any pretty clothes, and I haven't any place to entertain the group, so I just stayed out of things."

"Any place to entertain!" cried Jennifer. "Listen, if you knew how much we've wanted to have a hayride and a barn party, you'd think twice before you said anything. Do you suppose—"

"My grandparents would just love to have one," Lynn cried, her eyes shining like stars. "Grandmother's always asking why I don't invite some of my friends home."

Jennifer looked at her, amazed that she had ever thought Lynn's sweet, heart-shaped face plain or unattractive.

"Grandfather would let us take the horses and the big wagon—I'm a good driver. And we could have a taffy pull afterward in our big kitchen. It has a huge fireplace, so we could pop corn and toast marshmallows. What do you think of the idea?"

"What do I think of the idea!" sighed Jennifer. "It's perfect—simply perfect. And here you've had this all the time and never said a word about it. How could you be so selfish? Just wait until I tell Jack and all our friends."

Hand in hand the girls ran down the broad, curving stairway to the front hall. At the door Lynn turned, and with old-fashioned courtesy thanked mother for all she had done and for her visit to her grandmother.

"I couldn't have accepted all those lovely clothes if you hadn't spoken to grandmother about it," she ended. "But when you explained that Jennifer's cousin had sent them and that Jennifer wanted to share them with me, grandmother decided that you were being real neighborly. I can't tell you how much I appreciate not only the clothes but—but everything." Her voice died away, and mother saw tears in the brown eyes. She put her arm around the slender shoulders and kissed her.

"We're going to expect you often," mother said. "Jack and some of his friends are going to help with the farm work until your grandfather is well. That will give you more time for sharing some of the fine social activities in your class at school. Now, be sure to come again tomorrow for your last dress fitting, so that you'll be all ready for the party."

As the door closed behind the happiest girl in town, the next-to-the-happiest girl in town turned to look at her mother. "You fraud," she said lovingly.

"You darling old fraud. Here I thought I'd planned on helping Lynn by giving her some clothes. And all the time you'd arranged the whole thing. Jack was right. I might have known that my mother would take matters into her own hands." Her face sobered as she added, "But how did you know I'd offer to help Lynn, Mother? Suppose I hadn't. After all, I've done a lot of unkind talking about the Evil Eye. I'm ashamed whenever I think of it!"

Mother's eyes were very tender as she looked at Jennifer's bent head. "I knew that my girl wouldn't be unkind after she realized the true reasons for Lynn's actions." She put her hand under her daughter's chin and lifted her head. She looked straight into Jennifer's eyes as she added, "But the most important statement of all to remember is this: 'Look not on his countenance, or on the height of his stature...: for the Lord seeth not as man seeth; for man looketh on the outward appearance, but the Lord looketh on the heart.'" 1 Samuel 16:7.

Chapter 9
Boots for Manfred

"OH, LOOK. It's snowing. It's really snowing!" shouted Stephen. He hurried to the front door, Marilyn and Cedric crowding close at his heels.

"Who'd ever have believed that we'd have snow here in Western Oregon!" exclaimed Cedric. "Why, all we ever see in winter is rain, rain, and more rain. I can scarcely believe my eyes."

The three youngsters stared out in wonder at the thick snowflake swirls that the strong November wind slanted across their rapidly whitening lawn.

"Last night's paper said storms and perhaps snow," volunteered Marilyn, "so I guess the weatherman really knew what he was talking about. And am I glad! At last we'll have a chance to use that old sled of Aunt Stephanie's that grandma told us to bring home from Burns when we were over there last summer."

Stephen and Marilyn looked at each other with wide, shining eyes. Then they began to jump up and down, joyfully clapping their hands.

"Don't act so silly," groaned fourteen-year-old Cedric. "Whatever gave you the idea that you could coast on that small amount of snow? Why, you can

103

still see the green blades of grass. They aren't half covered yet."

"I don't see what difference that makes," sharply retorted Marilyn. "We can still drag the sled around the yard."

Cedric sighed wearily and looked with disdain at the two younger children. "Maybe Stephen doesn't know that you can't coast on a quarter-inch of snow. He's only a second-grader, but you're in the sixth. What do you learn in school, anyway?"

"Children, children," admonished mother as she hastily came in from the kitchen. "Please don't be rude, even in fun. Try to be as courteous to each other as you would be to a guest in our home."

She shivered as a strong gust of wind swirled a spray of icy crystals across the tiny porch and into the open doorway.

"Brr-rr! It certainly is cold. If the thermometer drops much more, we'll really have a siege of winter weather. Come inside and close the door. We'll watch from the living room window for a few moments."

"I think I'll go out for a little while and see what the snow feels like," Marilyn said. She hurried to the hall closet, grabbed her coat, scarf, and galoshes, and began hastily to pull them on. "I've always wished we'd have a really-truly snowstorm, and here it is."

"Some years ago we had a regular blizzard," mother answered, "but I guess you were too small to remember that."

"I'll remember this snowfall," smiled Marilyn as she kissed her mother's flushed cheek, and hurried outside to run in circles in the ever-thickening storm.

"Aren't you going out too?" questioned mother. She looked inquiringly at Stephen, whose happy face clouded over with a look of disappointment.

"I—I guess so. But I do wish that I had some boots to wear in the snow—real boots like Cedric's wearing right now."

Mother glanced quickly at Cedric as she put her hand on Stephen's rumpled hair. "Why, you do have some boots, and they are very nice ones, too, son. I don't know of anything better to keep your feet warm and dry than your new pair of three-fastener galoshes."

"Oh, sure, they're all right, I guess," Stephen burst forth disgustedly. "But I didn't want that kind in the first place. I told daddy I didn't when he bought them for me. I wanted a pair of real, high-topped laced boots like Cedric's. I'd just give anything to have a pair!"

The rebellious little boy's lip quivered and his brown eyes filled with hot tears that he hastily blinked back.

Mother looked understandingly down at him as she replied. "You mustn't make yourself unhappy by wishing for things that you don't really need, dear. Remember, Cedric earned his own clothing money this past summer, working hard picking fruit and harvesting beans. By doing so he was able to buy several pairs of shoes: one pair for church and dress wear, one pair for school, and his laced boots for school and play. But daddy felt that he could not afford to buy both galoshes and boots for you, and the galoshes seemed much more practical. Now run along and have a good time. I'll call you pretty soon."

All night the snow fell silently and thickly, covering the level spaces with a smooth white blanket and swirling into high roadside drifts. The children hurried to school, wrapped in its enveloping embrace, and ran home in a steady increase of wind and dancing snowflakes. Then for awhile they played in the front yard, making a huge snowman. Finally, they came in, rosy and smiling and as hungry as the proverbial three bears.

"Daddy has to go to a meeting this evening, so we're eating a little earlier than usual," mother said as they brushed off their snowy shoes in the entry and shook their coats and gloves before placing them on hangers by the stove. "I wanted you to have some extra playtime, so I didn't call you in to help me this time. Now hurry and wash your hands. I have a nice surprise for our worship hour."

The boys stood politely beside their chairs until mother and daddy and Marilyn were seated. Then they slipped quietly into their places and bowed their heads while daddy said grace.

"How good everything looks, Mother!" daddy remarked as he looked appreciatively at the attractively set table and began to serve generous portions of the sliced nut roast, mashed potatoes and gravy, creamed peas, and vegetable salad. "You don't realize how much I look forward to a well-cooked home meal. I hope our daughter is learning how to be a good cook. I can think of no greater accomplishment for a young lady."

Mother's eyes twinkled as she looked at Marilyn. "Well, this afternoon she had an important engagement with Mr. Snowman, but most of the time she's very faithful in her kitchen duties."

They had just finished their dinner and leaned back in their chairs when Cedric excused himself, left the table, and ran hastily upstairs.

"What is that boy—" began daddy, but the children saw mother knowingly shake her head and signal him to be silent. As rapidly as Cedric had left he returned. When they looked at him they saw that in his hands he carried a pair of sturdy, high-topped boots with strong rawhide laces and buckled straps.

"There you are, Stephen," he said gaily, placing them in his young brother's lap. "I'd been saving this pair of outgrown boots for a long time. I thought I'd give them to you for Christmas, for they're still almost as good as new. But since it's snowing I thought you'd probably enjoy them more right now. So put them on and we'll see how they fit!"

Stephen's excited gasp and his small, trembling fingers better expressed his delight than did his stammered thanks. He could scarcely fasten the laces and buckle the straps. Cedric helped him and then knelt to measure the length of his little brother's toes.

"Hm-m. Not much too long at that. You'll grow into them pretty fast. I guess it's a good thing I gave them to you now."

"O Cedric," Stephen exclaimed, "thank you! They—they're the most beautiful boots I ever saw. O Mother, may I put on my wraps and run outside for just a minute? Please, may I?"

At mother's smiling nod Stephen was gone. Dragging on his wraps as he ran through the doorway, he whistled to Cookie, the cocker spaniel, and then the two of them flung themselves into the ever deepening snow. Daddy and Cedric turned on the bright porch light and stood at the window to watch their excited romping while mother and Marilyn hurried to clear the table and scrape and stack the dishes before the worship hour.

"I'm glad you gave those boots to your little brother," said daddy, placing his arm across Cedric's shoulders. "A pair of boots has been his heart's desire for a long time, and he will enjoy those particular ones more than anything else you could have given him. It won't be long until he'll be able to wear them to school, and how proud he will be then!"

At the beginning of the worship hour Stephen settled himself beside Cedric on the davenport, booted feet sticking straight out in front of him in the direct line of his admiring look.

"Didn't you say that you had a surprise for us tonight, Mother? Or did you mean the boots?" questioned Marilyn as mother sat down.

"No, the boots were a surprise to me as well as to you," mother smilingly announced. "But I really do have another surprise. Can you guess what it is?"

She held up a cream-colored envelope decorated in one corner with the small picture of a horse and rider. Everyone stared blankly at the familiar-looking envelope with its strange script and foreign stamp. Stephen was the first to move. He flashed across the room to look closely at the letter.

"Is it one of the envelopes we sent to Manfred, Mother?" he asked. "It looks just the same. Oh, is it a letter from him?"

Mother put her arm around the excited little boy and hugged him close. "Yes, this is some of the writing paper that we mailed to this refugee family in Germany. You will remember that their name was sent to us by our General Conference headquarters in Washington, D.C., after we had written to the Home Missionary secretary and requested the names and addresses of four needy European families.

"Well, this is the first answer that we have received since we sent away our home-packed boxes to them, and I'm going to read it for worship. It was written by Manfred's mother. I'm sure that you will find it very interesting.

"'GREETINGS, OUR DEAR BRETHREN IN THE DISTANCE:

"'On Friday we received the so-precious package. Omchen [grandmother] had gone with Manfred to Emden to get wooden shoes for the little boy who has been ill with scarlet fever and a sore throat, because he had not any shoes the whole winter, and therefore could not go to school. When I heard that I had a package to receive, oh, how excited and nervous I became. Yes, also at this moment our benefactors should have seen how with beaming eyes we carried the package to our house under our arm. The small package "To a Little Boy" I left for Manfred. You are so far from us, but it seems to me that you stood before me, and that I could in thankfulness clasp your hand. Finally we are

109

here, and then came the most beautiful moment. How can we thank you? I can say that the Lord Jesus already blessed your hands when you were packing the package, so that all of the things fit for us. The mittens, too, fit and the red light [candle] is serviceable for us, for we are often without lights.

"'When he saw the mint sticks [candy canes] he sprang high into the air; and the tiny autos and ship, he got more and more excited. And the best of all was that which he has had to do without for so long-chocolate. "Ah," he said, "how dear the aunt is! She has a heart for children." He has wished for toys for himself, and now the Lord Jesus has heard his wish.

"'The little boy went to sleep at eleven o'clock. He said, "I cannot go to sleep. I can only shake my head. The beautiful things! I have prayed the Saviour that He would send me some playthings from America. Now I have received so much!"

"'I'm glad that I now have stockings for Sabbath. I thank you especially for the warm underwear and clothing, for here by the water it is so damp cold with few covers and the cement floor.

"'Victuals are scarce, and the things that you sent will strengthen us: the milk and yellow corn meal, the red beans and bags with sugar. Of your precious things I have given some to my sister. Life is hard, and the need is great, but God's help is greater. This we have experienced again. Accept our thanks, which comes from the heart, our dear benefactors. May the Lord for your so great love bless you in rich measure. We can only say "Thank you—thank you—thank you!"

"'We wish you God's strength, help, and blessing, and may He us prepare that He can come soon in the clouds of heaven. May He give us mercy, that we shall reach the highest aim and that there we shall find you and our thanks shall be joy. (Isaiah 33:22)'"

Everyone was very still as mother's quavering voice finished. Then daddy cleared his throat, Cedric lowered his head, and Marilyn and Stephen wiped their brimming eyes.

"You mean—you mean that Manfred can't even go to school because he hasn't any *shoes*? And he's had both scarlet fever and an infected throat and has to go bare-footed in the cold?" Stephen gasped in horror.

"I'm afraid so," mother nodded soberly. "As she says in the postscript, they're right on the border between Germany and Holland, and the winters are severely damp and cold. Think, children, of having not only no shoes but no underclothing, very little food, and only enough bedding to make a pallet on the cement floor. We simply cannot realize the suffering undergone by these poor people who have been driven out of their homeland, leaving all their possessions behind them."

"Since he's traced around his foot and sent his shoe size, perhaps down at the Dorcas room you can find a pair of shoes that will fit him," daddy suggested.

"I'll certainly try," mother answered dubiously, "but all of the shoes that come in are oxfords, and well-worn ones at that. And since Manfred particularly needs high shoes, I'm afraid that we can't help him much in that respect."

111

"You Mean—You Mean That Manfred Can't Even Go
to School Because He Hasn't Any Shoes?"

"Couldn't you buy a pair?" asked Marilyn, wide-eyed with sympathy.

Mother slowly shook her head. "No, dear, I'm afraid not. You see, boots are now very expensive—at least $12 or more a pair, and I can't afford to pay such a high price. We'll just have to wait and hope that we can find someone who is willing to donate a pair."

After prayer the children went quietly to their rooms and prepared for bed. And as mother tucked them in for the night she knew from one good-night hug and kiss that one little heart carried an extra heavy burden.

Both at breakfast time the next day and during the evening dinner and worship hour Stephen remained unusually still.

"What's wrong, son? Don't you feel well?" daddy anxiously inquired. "You haven't spoken a dozen words all evening, and that's something unheard-of for our chatterbox. Perhaps we should get out some of the medicine prescribed by our doctor. I certainly hope you aren't going to be ill. We don't want another hospital siege!"

"Oh, no, Daddy, I'm all right. Really I am," Stephen answered quickly. "It's just that—well, it's just—I've been thinking that perhaps I should send my new boots over to Manfred, so he can go to school. He doesn't have any shoes at all, and I have two pairs and my warm galoshes. I do like the boots just lots better than the galoshes, though." A salty tear rolled down his red cheek as his choked little voice stopped abruptly; he brushed it away with the back of his hand.

113

Daddy swallowed hard and tightened his grip on Stephen's hands, but he remained silent as Stephen concluded, "Do you think Jesus will think I'm selfish if I still miss my boots after I send them away? I want Manfred to have them; I really do, but—but—" The small voice grew fainter and fainter until only a sharp aching sob spoke more eloquently than words could have done.

"No, son, I don't believe that Jesus will think you are selfish if you still miss your boots," said daddy, drawing him close in his embrace. "That's the most wonderful thing about our Saviour. He always understands."

"Never mind, Stevie," soothed Cedric, getting up from his chair and walking over to his tearful brother. "I'll tell you what I'll do. I'll save this pair that I'm wearing. Of course they're too large now, but I'll outgrow them before long. Then I'll grease them and put them away for you, and in another few years you'll be able to wear them. That'll be something for you to look forward to, now, won't it?" He patted Stephen's shoulder as his little brother gave a shaky laugh.

"Stephen, I think your idea is wonderful," affirmed mother. "And I have the very box to put them in, with some of the Christmas paper and stickers and red ribbon left over from last year. We'll add some shortening, cocoa, creamed honey, sugar, lentils, breakfast cereals, dried fruits, and canned milk. We'll add soap, needles, thread, and darning cotton, too, for our General Conference stated that these poor people lacked all these articles."

"I'm going to let you pack and wrap the box this very evening, write your own name on a card, and mail the gifts to Manfred for his Christmas present."

Sorrow forgotten in the joy of doing something for others, Stephen spent the following half hour in polishing and wrapping his boots. Next came the packing of the other articles, assisted by Marilyn and Cedric. The last gifts to be tucked in were two of Stephen's best picture books. Finally came the fun of carefully tying the box with heavy cord and filling out the mailing tags. And the very next day after school Stephen and Marilyn went downtown to the post office and proudly paid overseas postage on the heavy twenty-one-pound package that daddy carried in for them.

Day after day Stephen played in the snow, wearing his galoshes. If at times he thought wistfully of his lost boots, he told himself that surely Manfred needed them far more than he himself ever would.

At last, on a never-to-be-forgotten afternoon, the second letter arrived. This message was also carefully written on one of the familiar looking envelops with the corner picture of the horse and rider. But this letter was addressed, in a careful childish handwriting, to:

SCHOLAR STEPHEN HAYDEN
Lake Street at Spring Boulevard
Eugene, Oregon
U.S.A.

"For me!" gasped Stephen. "A letter from Germany for *me*!" Carefully he cut a narrow slice from the end of the envelope and pulled out the

115

bulky letter. He opened it up, and there, folded in the note of thanks from Manfred, was a picture of a dark-haired, dark-eyed boy about his own age, smiling right at him.

"Read it. Please hurry up and read what he says," urged Marilyn. "I can hardly wait."

Quickly he read aloud the polite, quaintly phrased little note, and after that they listened eagerly to the letter from Manfred's mother. Over and over the children read and reread certain paragraphs until they could recite them by heart.

"'The dear gift parcel you sent us we received on Thursday with a great joy. How can we thank you for all your love? All was so nicely packed in, and we were happy. It is a pity we cannot say thanks ourselves.

"'Our little Manfred is overjoyed for the shoes and the stockings. Now he can again go to school. Oh, the fun was great when he sees the boots and

A Letter for Stephen Hayden

116

also the picture books. And how much Manfred is pleased for the story of Jesus and the Bible stories. The children in America do have it so nice that they can get all these nice things.

"'Many greetings to the dear children, especially from Manfred, who is so happy over his things. And many greetings and God's blessing from your thankful friends and Manfred.'"

Stephen lifted shining brown eyes and looked around the family circle. "Oh!" he exclaimed, "how glad I am that I sent those Christmas presents overseas. It's really wonderful to know that we helped others; isn't it, mother?"

"Indeed it is, dear," nodded mother. "And we must continue to do all we can to help this needy family, who, like many others, have lost everything."

"I'll look around and sort out some of my old clothes that I've outgrown," added Cedric enthusiastically. "Even if they're too large, his mother can cut them down and make them the right size for him."

"It'll be nice to send more boxes," happily agreed Stephen as he looked down proudly at the picture and letter held carefully in his hands. "But somehow I don't think I'll ever have so much fun out of giving away anything else as I did when sending overseas my boots for Manfred.

"You Do Have a Sad and Doleful Appearance Today," Teased Ann

Chapter 10
Junior Dorcas, Unlimited

"WHAT'S WRONG, Maebelle? You look as sour as a lemon." Lois laughed merrily as she hurried out the hall door after her friend. The morning recess bell had just rung, and the girls were determined not to waste one second of the midwinter sunshine.

"I agree with Lois. You do have a sad and doleful appearance today," teased Ann. "Is anything wrong? Did you get a low grade in that last algebra examination? Surely nothing else could cause such a look of woe."

Maebelle tossed her thick, dark curls defiantly. "Oh, all right, everybody. Go ahead and make fun of me if you want to; I don't care. I got exactly 98 in that algebra test, and nothing's wrong with me. It's just that—oh, everything seems so dull. I do the same old things every day—get up, make my bed, eat breakfast, come to school, study, go home, practice, set the table, eat, do dishes, go to bed. And—"

"Why don't you save time and energy, and leave out the meals, then?" added Winona, who, arm in arm with Janet, had joined the small group.

"Sometimes I just about feel like leaving out everything, especially when I'm told that I have to help with some extra church work. I don't mind doing my part, but when it comes to Family Dorcas night, I think that's just too much to expect!"

"Family Dorcas? What's that?" questioned Winona. "I've never heard of that before. Don't you mean the Dorcas society that meets regularly one afternoon a week in the church basement? Mother goes to that whenever she can, or takes some of the sewing and mending home to do."

"No, I don't mean Dorcas; I mean Family Dorcas. It's some new project they've just started. The men and women meet in the school dining hall and pack boxes to send overseas. The ladies do the sorting and packing, and label the tags, and then the men rope the boxes and seal them with heavy tape. My folks are going tonight, and so of course I have to go too. I'll be bored to death—I know I will."

"I don't blame you. I would too," sympathized Lois and Winona.

"I won't. I think it'll be fun," spoke up one of the younger girls, who had just stopped to hear the discussion. "Mother said that I could go along and help pack a box for a refugee family who used to live in Russia. They were dreadfully persecuted there and had to flee for their lives. The man spent two years in exile in Siberia. Now they live with about thirty other Adventists in a little village near the Russian border. They have scarcely any clothing at all, except what they have on. And they have scarcely any food, either."

"How did your mother get all that information, Marilyn?" asked Bethene, as the older girls, somewhat interested in spite of themselves, looked at Marilyn's eager face. "Some of us were out of town last week, and we didn't hear your mother's talk in the Home Missionary service. I overheard my folks mention it, though, and they said that she explained about the relief work that's being done."

"Well," began Marilyn, "last fall mother wrote to the Home Missionary Department of our General Conference headquarters in Washington, D.C., and asked for the names of two needy families. You see, Stephen and I had been saving our outgrown clothing for some time. We'd decided to 'adopt' a family or two overseas, so that we could send them boxes of food and clothing, and write to them. In a short time mother had an answer. But when we checked on the names we found that neither family had young children. Then she wrote again and asked for the names of two more families. Now we have twenty on our own personal list."

"I can't see why you have to have children of a certain age," stated Ann. "What difference does that make?"

"Why, because our clothing wouldn't fit the older folks. But now we have three little girls, Lina, Adina, and Anna, and two or three little boys, and we can send all our good used clothing to them. But we'll have to send much more, because these four families have sent the names of many poor relatives and friends. Now we have more than ninety names on the complete list, and that is why the Family Dorcas group has been organized."

"Are they really that poor?" curiously asked Evelyn. "I thought that tons and tons of supplies had been sent overseas. I simply can't imagine people so destitute that they don't even have shoes."

"Why don't you girls come tonight?" urged Marilyn. "I can't answer all your questions, but mother can. This week she received some more letters from Germany; she's going to read two or three of them at the meeting. Please try to come, and bring Maebelle with you. I'd hate to see her die from boredom. This will be a change from the same old routine at least."

The group disbanded with merry laughs at Maebelle's expense, but her sunny disposition proved equal to the test, and she only smiled at their friendly teasing.

When Maebelle reached the dining room that evening, she found most of the girls already there. Some were busily at work sorting out the large piles of groceries that had been brought in response to the pleas for a "Pound Night" for the Family Dorcas. However, generous friends had not limited their offerings to a pound of food. The surprised girls noted large packages of beans, rice, dried peas, lentils, sugar, honey, corn meal, oatmeal, vegetable shortening, chocolate, malted milk, dried fruits, powdered milk, and soap. They saw many sturdy boxes filled with good used clothing, clean and mended, and ready to be sorted for shipping. One box contained shoes for men, women, and children.

"Did you bring all these things from the church Dorcas room?" Yvonne asked Mrs. Robertson, the Dorcas leader.

"Oh, no," Mrs. Robertson hastily answered. "These were all given in response to our call for extra help; we always work each Thursday afternoon on our local relief program for the needy around

us in our own community. No, many of these garments came from friends in other churches who are
interested in our direct contact with these needy
overseas folk. In fact, we're getting so many contri-
butions that we have to meet an extra evening now
and then in order to keep ahead of our donations."
She smiled at their look of astonished surprise and
then continued:

"Perhaps you girls would like to choose several
names and pack boxes for those particular families.
We have found that the most efficient way to pack is
to form a three-man team: one person to sort out the
articles, one person to pack them, and one person to
list each article and its cost on the two tags required
for attaching to the box. It's quite an undertaking,
as you'll discover before the evening is over.

"Marilyn's mother has the complete list with the
names, ages, and birthdays of each needy member of the household. Now, decide which family you
want to choose, and by consulting the list you will
be able to pack the box to the very best advantage."

"How much can we put in each package, Mrs.
Robertson?" questioned Maebelle, interested in
spite of her gloomy forecast for the evening.

"You'll have to remember that, according to
the present postal regulations, each box must not
weigh over twenty-two pounds when it is packed,
tagged, sealed, and roped. Some of us learned the
hard way, and had to bring back our first packages
from the post office and take out several articles in
order not to exceed the weight allowed. Then another important point is that every box must be packed
tightly so that nothing rattles or moves around in it.

"I'd suggest that each of you try to imagine what you would need most of all if you were a refugee—a person who was homeless or forced out of his own home into whatever shelter he could find."

"Put out of your own home!" exclaimed Maebelle. "Do they really do that to people? Why, how do they exist?"

As the girls selected several names and portioned out suitable clothing and food for the families chosen, they listened to accounts of the conditions among the refugees who had already received boxes sent by the Family Dorcas and kind friends.

"Is it possible that there are still good and kind people in the world who care what happens to us? How can we ever repay you? We cannot repay you, but the Almighty will repay you both in this life and in eternity. To you all many thanks once more and God's blessing and grace from your brothers and sisters in the Lord. (Romans 8:35-39; Titus 3:15)" Thus wrote one lady.

"For two years I was exiled in Siberia," wrote one father. "It has been so long since my little girls had shoes that I do not know what size they wear. Therefore I am sending slips of paper upon which are the lengths of their feet. I have neither a summer shirt nor a winter shirt, and we all sleep without bedding. We receive just enough food to keep us from starving to death. Any help that you can possibly give us will be so much appreciated. We have suffered much. But though we are so poor in earthly goods we are rich in heavenly faith."

The girls' fingers fairly flew after the reading of the letters. And Maebelle's hands moved faster than any. Over and over she silently repeated to herself, "We all sleep without bedding—no underclothing—just enough food to keep us from starving."

What joy it was to pack a fluffy, blue wool blanket in the bottom of the box for that particular family. How happy she felt as she helped to weigh and sort out the beans, rice, sugar, chocolate, shortening, and other foodstuffs that would aid those poor sufferers on the long road back to health. As she added needles, thread, darning cotton, shoelaces, soap—all the small but necessary articles unobtainable overseas—she felt as if she were doing it for well-known friends. It was hard to decide what to put in and what to leave out, for the telltale scales kept mounting up, up. But the girls at last decided to put in warm dresses and coats, and leave the heavy shoes for the next time. And last, but by no means least, to the three little girls who would so happily receive them, went in three wee plastic dolls in tiny blue and pink cradles—toys so dear to the hearts of children the world around.

It was 10:30 when Mrs. Robertson called out a cheery "Time's up for the evening," and they all began to put away the many articles left for the next shipment.

"Where has the time gone?" exclaimed Maebelle, looking up in surprised dismay. "Why, it seems as if we came only a few minutes ago."

"What!" Marilyn teased. "Aren't you the girl who was so afraid of being bored? I expected to find you in tears before the evening ended."

"You almost did," soberly assented Maebelle. "I nearly shed tears over some of those letters. I'm more ashamed than I can say over my silly attitude today complaining about being bored. But I honestly didn't know that there were such people. What in the world have I to complain about when I have everything a girl ever needed?"

"I'm going home to start looking over my old clothes and mending them so that they, too, can be sent abroad. And—"

"O girls, look what Joyce brought tonight," excitedly interrupted Marilyn. "It was tucked away behind this big box, and no one saw it back there in the corner. Aren't these things just darling?"

With excited oh's and ah's they inspected the eighty-three beautiful little garments for a small girl. Some of the articles had never been worn, and all the others were in excellent condition and daintily laundered, ready for use.

"Wouldn't it be fun if we could organize a Girls' Club and 'adopt' a family or two of our own?" asked Bethene enthusiastically. "There were several families listed who had four or five little children. We could send these clothes and make others. I noticed that one mother had a tiny baby. Why couldn't we make a complete layette? I made a doll layette as a gift for a little neighbor girl, but it would be so much more useful to make one for an actual baby, and I just love to sew."

"Yes, and we could make some of those cunning rag dolls and teddy bears and stuffed elephants that Bethene's and Yvonne's mothers make. I know they'd help us. We could send them overseas for Christmas and birthday presents," volunteered Winona. "How those little kiddies would love them!

Just think—they have never had even one single toy! Oh, I think it would be so much fun."

"I do to," agreed Maebelle, "and that's the answer to my problem right there. I need to do more for others and forget myself. We can meet regularly at our homes and work out a definite project. But let's not call this a Girl's Club. I think I have a better name than that to suggest. Come over here and see what you think of this idea. Here, I'll write it down."

The older Dorcas members looked with misty eyes as the girls' excited voices rose higher and higher in their last-minute plans.

"Bless them. They don't know what a lot of good they can do with their hopeful young hearts and their willing hands," said Mrs. Robertson.

"And they don't know how much good it's going to do all of us," softly added Maebelle to the girls, from their unintentional listening post in the upstairs hall. "Why, there's no limit to the good that we can do right here at home as well as abroad. From now on we'll really show some friendly competition to Family Dorcas. Yes, girls, I predict great things for Junior Dorcas, *Unlimited*."

We invite you to view the complete
selection of titles we publish at:

www.TEACHServices.com

Scan with your mobile
device to go directly
to our website.

Please write or email us your praises, reactions, or
thoughts about this or any other book we publish at:

TEACH Services, Inc.
PUBLISHING
www.TEACHServices.com ✎ (800) 367-1844

P.O. Box 954
Ringgold, GA 30736

info@TEACHServices.com

TEACH Services, Inc., titles may be purchased in bulk
for educational, business, fund-raising, or sales pro-
motional use. For information, please e-mail:

BulkSales@TEACHServices.com

Finally, if you are interested in seeing
your own book in print, please contact us at

publishing@TEACHServices.com

We would be happy to review your manuscript for free.

CPSIA information can be obtained at www.ICGtesting.com
Printed in the USA
BVOW03s1212101014

370079BV00010B/109/P

9 781479 601080